I0610565

CUPID'S REVENGE

NAUGHTY CUPID SERIES ANNIVERSARY EDITION

MICHELLE M PILLOW

MICHELLEPILLOW.COM

Cupid's Revenge (Naughty Cupid) © copyright 2005-2019, Michelle M. Pillow

Revised Anniversary Edition July 2019, The Raven Books LLC

Second Electronic Printing July 2010

First Electronic Printing September 2005

Cover art © Copyright 2019 Book Cover Media

ISBN-13: 978-1-62501-248-7

ISBN-10: 1-62501-248-9

ALL RIGHTS RESERVED.

All books copyrighted to the author and may not be resold or given away without written permission from the author, Michelle M. Pillow.

This novel is a work of fiction. Any and all characters, events, and places are of the author's imagination and should not be confused with fact. Any resemblance to persons, living or dead, or events or places is merely coincidence. Novel intended for adults only. Must be 18 years or older to read.

Michelle M. Pillow® is a registered trademark of The Raven Books LLC

Cupid's Revenge
Paranormal Fantasy Romance
Naughty Cupid Book Two

Cupid's livid. It's bad enough he made two people fall in love, but now thanks to King Larus, the whole Immortal Realm knows about it. There's only one thing a troll can do. Get Revenge.

Lady Mina and her sister are impoverished, starving, and their castle home is crumbling around their feet. With their father is dead, the servants have all fled and left them to fend for themselves in the middle of winter. Mina doesn't think things could get worse, until they're kidnapped and left as an offering to a handsome man-beast.

After Cupid caused a great disruption amongst his lycans by bringing an enchanted human to their realm, King Larus had to meet with the Council of Elders to tell what the troll had done. It should have been enough to stop future mischief. Or so he thought. Now he's trapped in the woods with two beautiful women—one whose madly in love with him and one who wants nothing more than to claw his eyes out. Larus is quickly learning not to underestimate a troll bent on revenge.

Author recommends reading books in order of release.
For details please visit www.michellepillow.com

*To those who don't like Valentine's Day—a Cupid even
you can love.*

Cupid's Enchantment
Cupid's Revenge
Cupid's Favor

MICHELLE'S BESTSELLING SERIES

QURILIXEN WORLD NOVELS

Dragon Lords Series
Barbarian Prince
Perfect Prince
Dark Prince
Warrior Prince
His Highness The Duke
The Stubborn Lord
The Reluctant Lord
The Impatient Lord
The Dragon's Queen

Lords of the Var® Series
The Savage King

The Playful Prince
The Bound Prince
The Rogue Prince
The Pirate Prince

Qurilixen Lords
Dragon Prince
More Coming Soon!

Captured by a Dragon-Shifter Series
Determined Prince
Rebellious Prince
Stranded with the Cajun
Hunted by the Dragon
Mischievous Prince
Headstrong Prince

Space Lords Series
His Frost Maiden
His Fire Maiden

His Metal Maiden
His Earth Maiden
His Woodland Maiden - Coming Soon

Dynasty Lords Series
Seduction of the Phoenix
Temptation of the Butterfly

Having trouble finding the books?
Updated Buy Links Here

To learn more about the Qurilixen World series of books
and to stay up to date on the latest book list visit
www.MichellePillow.com

AUTHOR UPDATES

Join the Reader Club Mailing List to stay informed about new books, sales, contests and preorders!

http://michellepillow.com/author-updates/

Curse the lycans.

Cupid's little black eyes flashed with an inner fire. And damn the council of immortal elders. So what if he took his vengeance out on Ilar by entrancing the whole Lycan Guard at Lycaon to one mortal woman? It's not like anyone had gotten hurt. Besides, Ilar, Commander of the Guard, deserved it for making fun of a noble troll—just as he deserved to be forced to lifemate to an ugly human woman.

Cupid shivered in disgust to think of how his plan had backfired. Ilar had fallen in love with the hideous mortal and they were living their fairy tale, happily ever after. It was disgustingly romantic. It was hideously repulsive. It was unbearable to think about.

Bah. Ach.

Now he had to listen to the other trolls tease him each time he saw them. They called him a cherub, a matchmaker, a rosy-faced babe who spread love and goodness throughout the two realms. If he had another basket of love darts left outside his cave door, he'd scream so loud the whole realm of magic would collapse in on itself.

Bah. Bah. Double bah.

Cupid hated the elders. He hated goodness and happiness. He hated Ilar and his ugly human lifemate, Rhiannon. He hated the council. He hated the realm of magic and the realm of mortals. He hated everyone and everything.

And, above all things, he hated love.

His humiliation wouldn't have been so widely known if the council of immortal elders hadn't been called forth. He blamed Larus, the elected king of the lycans, for that one. It was Larus's court at Lycaon that had been affected by his small enchantment prank. He merely made the mortal woman irresistible to the lycan kind and brought the whole court howling to their knees with lust.

But, could the lycan king let it go? No. He had to draw attention to the fact that Cupid had found love for Lord Ilar and Lady Rhiannon. He had to tell everyone who would listen to him that Cupid was personally responsible for Ilar's eternal happiness.

Now Cupid would never live his reputation down. First, he *accidentally* hit a man instead of a goat with a love dart, causing *one* couple to fall in love four hundred years ago, and now this. He was going to be branded for his immortal life as a matchmaker. It was beyond torture, beyond fair and right, beyond tolerable.

And, as far as Cupid could determine, it was King Larus who needed to pay for that.

LYCAON CASTLE, REALM OF MAGIC

King Larus watched Lady Rhiannon with her lifemate, Lord Ilar. They seemed truly happy together, and he was pleased for them. Ilar was his best soldier, a great leader, and a true friend. He deserved happiness. But the fact that Rhiannon was human still made him uneasy.

Even though he liked Rhiannon, Larus hoped she would be the last human he saw in his eternity of living. Humans had killed his family—his parents, brothers, sisters and cousins until all he had left was his duty to his people. He did his duty with pride and dedication. For nearly a hundred and fifty years he'd been their ruler and, so long as they willed it, he would remain their elected king.

"Did the elders decide what to do with Cupid?" Ilar asked, coming near the head table of the empty council hall. "Will he be punished for opening a portal?"

King Larus looked up, gazing past the giant circular pit of flames that lit the room. He sat atop a long stone table, scratching thoughtfully at the back of his head. Slowly, he lowered his arms to lie on top of his crossed legs. He came to the hall often, especially when he needed to be alone and think. When it was empty, the room was complete silence, aside from the soft rustling of the fire pit.

"Naturally, they aren't pleased with what he has done," Larus stated after a time.

Cupid was a squat little troll and like all of his kind he had a horrible temper backed by extreme power. Trolls had no real allegiance to anyone, let alone mortals, and only used their magic for self-gain or mischief. They wouldn't open the portals to humankind just so the mortals could flood into their world. No, they'd only open them for their selfish reasons. Their stupid, narcissistic ways could end up being the downfall of the entire realm of immortals.

Larus had been outraged to discover Cupid had opened up the portal between the mortal realm and the magic realm. He didn't want to relive the wars between the mortal and immortal. They'd fought once, long ago, and there'd been much death on both sides. In the end, it was decided the realms should be forever separated. That was why the portals had been sealed. That was why they had to remain sealed.

Only a few natural portals remained, as they couldn't be destroyed. The doors on the mortal side were locked with the strong magic and charms of all immortal races. The only way the portals could be opened was from their side. But once opened, the realms could merge freely.

Cupid had broken the pact of the covenants that protected the magic realm from human greed for the last three hundred years. The risk of humans wandering back through was too significant. It was a risk none of the elders were willing to take.

The lycans weren't the only ones to leave the world of mortal men. The vampires, who were also hunted because of their 'unnatural' ways, had come with them as did all things of magic—elves, fairies, even the goblins and dwarfs. They left the humans, tired of being trapped and forced to use magic for mankind's gain. Then it was believed that humans would kill themselves off. It wasn't to be so. To everyone's amazement, the humans thrived. And, until Cupid's little play of revenge against Lord Ilar, the realms had remained separated.

Larus glanced at Lady Rhiannon and smiled faintly. They were the only three in the hall and he knew, since she was lifemated to Ilar, he could speak freely before her. "Though the outcome is good, what could have been is beyond forgiveness. Cupid risked too much over a petty insult."

Lord Ilar had drunkenly offended Cupid one night by calling him a rosy-faced cherub. That in and of itself was comical. Cupid's wrinkled face was anything but rosy and, with the horrible smell he emitted from his foul, unwashed body, he didn't come close to reminding them of a cherub.

Cupid, however, obviously didn't see the humor in the jests. So to get even, the troll had gone to the realm of the mortals, doused Lady Rhiannon in magical lycan pheromone to enchant her and brought her to their world. The mere smell of her had sent the entire unmated population into a desperate, lustful frenzy.

The males of the Lycaon court had fought like madmen to possess Rhiannon and the women had fought to kill her. Because of the raging emotions, their telepathic mind link had been blocked. The mind link was the only way the lycan could communicate in their shifted form and they used it often to warn of attacks. Without it, their defenses were left weakened. Both Ilar and Larus had feared they were under magical assault until they discovered the real reason.

Knowing it was only a troll's petty revenge that

opened the portals and caused the disruption in his guards, Larus frowned. Cupid risked too much, but then trolls weren't known for their consideration of consequences. As king, he'd been honor bound to report Cupid's actions to the council. The troll was in some serious trouble.

"Death seems too harsh of a punishment and yet I feel, with Cupid, anything less would fail to make an impact on his troll brain," Ilar said.

"Well," Rhiannon offered softly, pushing her long, curly blonde hair over her shoulder. She looked more lycan than human as she wore the comfortable gown of his people—a large square piece of cloth that was wrapped around the body and secured with a clasp at the shoulder. Though, instead of leaving her body bare beneath, she wore an undergarment with long sleeves. Being as she was human, the slight modification allowed her extra protection against the elements. Her blue eyes looked first to her husband and then back to Larus. "At least he won't be opening the portal again, will he?"

"The council has ordered him not to bring back any more enchanted humans," Larus said. "Although, they're unsure what to do with him otherwise. Because no troll sits on the council, we can only do so much."

"Then, he's agreed not to enchant any more humans?" Ilar asked, his dark eyes steady.

"Yes, he's agreed," Larus answered. "I believe him. I think Lady Rhiannon's and your happiness is punishment enough. By the time I got done telling the council, and everyone else who would listen, about his good deed, he was thoroughly mortified. Word of your love has even leaked to the trolls. If I know that race, they will persecute him enough to ensure he never does anything so foolish again."

2

WESSEX, REALM OF MORTALS, WINTER 1407 AD

Cupid looked out over the ruins of an empty human keep and frowned. Winter snow lay thick and white over the crumbling walls of the castle, blanketing the abandoned bailey yard. A battering ram had decimated the iron bars of the front gate, and by the holes in the high towers it could be assumed a catapult had flung boulders at the stone. This place had been attacked.

Why would his magic bring him to an abandoned mortal keep? Cupid frowned, slowly scratching his backside in thought.

"I don't want to hear it, Sophia," a slender human woman yelled, coming from inside the crumbling mortal home.

Cupid grimaced at the sound. The human had long black hair and light brown eyes that he could see clearly from his spot on the wall. He jumped down to get a closer look at her, not sure he wanted to. Aye, she was an ugly creature—skin smooth without any flaws, two arched brows, and hair that shone with an inner gleam. *Ach.* Not a wrinkle or pustule to be seen and not a single mole. How was it humans could breed with such hideous creatures as these? It was a wonder the race didn't wither away due to complete and utter repulsion.

He knew the hideous human couldn't see him, as he was cloaked with magic, so he crept closer. He continued to scratch his gnarled hand absently at his inflamed backside. When his short fingers didn't quite get the itch through the filthy material of his breeches, he dug his hand beneath his pants and scraped his nails over the sores he found there. A small sigh left his lips, even as the scratching burned.

Suddenly, a waft of clean human flesh assaulted him and he gagged. Pulling his hand from his pants, he shoved two fingers up his oversized nose to block the nauseating stench. Shaking his head, he shivered. If he weren't so mad at the lycan king, he'd never be able to stay in the ugly woman's presence.

Ach. Revenge was ugly work indeed.

However, remembering the fresh basket of love darts left before his cave and the bundle of sweet-smelling flowers that some magical creature had thrown into his den, he stiffened his resolve. Someone had to pay for that. And that someone was King Larus.

3

"I don't want to hear it, Sophia."

Lady Mina of Aucester tossed her dark hair over her shoulder and turned to watch her sister come from the castle. White puffs of air came with the words and her cheeks stung with the coldness of the winter day. She shivered, drawing her worn cloak tightly around her body. Sophia made a small sound of discomfort and did the same.

Sophia could well have been her twin, except that she was a few years younger and instead of hair as black as night, she had locks as gold as the sun. Their faces were nearly identical, down to the shape of their brown eyes and the tilt of their noses. They were the same height and the same slender build. Their lips were full, the interest of many men—men who'd wanted to marry them before their father's execution and now who wanted them as their whores after it.

"I don't care if you don't want to hear it, Mina. The facts remain the same, whether we say them or not. We're impoverished noblewomen whose father was marked as a conspirator against the king. It's not like anyone even cares that we exist. We could die on the morn and not one person would shed a tear, except the poor bastard who had to cart off our stinking, rotting corpses. And that is even if they bother to do that much." Sophia lifted her chin. "It has been nearly two years since our father's death. Not one person has come for us. This isn't even our land anymore. King Henry will most likely award it to a loyal knight. What do you think will happen when that loyal sir gets here and sees us waiting around?"

"I know." Mina said, hating the words even as she knew they were true. Trying to calm herself, she said in a softer tone, "I know, Sophia. He'll make us his whores. You've said it so many times, how can I not know it? But this is our home. Where else have we to go? You want to leave, but to where? We have no one, nothing. We have not been anywhere else, at least not beyond the traveling market. And the king may have seized it, but this is still our land, our home. This is where we were born."

"And I do not want this to be where we die." Sophia gave her sister a mournful look. Her arms lifted at her sides as she gestured around them helplessly. "Mina, look at this place. It's in ruins. I don't even recognize it anymore. Please. Please, for me. Let us leave this awful place. We have our title, tarnished as it is. We have our education. We have each other. We're still ladies."

Mina knew Sophia meant well, but it didn't make her words any easier to hear. Looking down, she picked at her chapped hands through the gloves. She was the oldest, which made her responsible for her sister. Quietly, she asked, "Where would you have us go? For once we are on the road we won't be able to eat our tarnished title of nobility and our education will not save us. It won't keep us warm and sheltered from the winter snows. Here we have shelter and, though it be scarce, we have food enough to survive."

"Survive? Mina, who wants to just survive? This is our chance," Sophia exclaimed. "We have waited for two years. We are forgotten."

"Our chance for what, sister?"

"Freedom," Sophia said, desperately. "True freedom. We are under no man's rule. Can't you feel it? We can do or say whatever we please, for life can't get any worse than it already has. Let us take it. Let us take our freedom."

Mina saw her little sister's eyes flash with excitement. A wave of grief overcame her. She didn't want to leave home. She loved it.

No, Mina thought mournfully, *that isn't necessarily true anymore. I love what it once was. I love what is no longer here. I love the past.*

She lifted her eyes to the light blue of the sky, to the white, puffy clouds that mimicked her breath. She shivered, feeling overwhelmed, feeling alone and scared. The tower that once stood so proud against the heavens had fallen—just like everything else in their lives. So many nights she lay awake, wishing she'd taken some offer of marriage—any offer. But no. At the time of the proposal, the offers had been beneath her. How foolish she was. How very vain. Now, she was paying for that vanity.

"Damn politics and damn the men who make them." Mina took a deep breath. Then, turning to her expectant sister, she said louder, "All right, Sophia, all right. I give up. If you wish to, we'll go. You're right. The servants have abandoned us. The knights have all gone to serve the king. Food is scarce. There is nothing left for us here and no one is coming."

Sophia grinned. She hopped up and down in excitement. Hope shone from her eyes. "Thank you, Mina, thank you. You'll see. Life will only get better once we are away for it can hardly get worse."

Cupid clapped his hands in glee and snorted in wild excitement. He laughed, happily doing a small jig. This was too perfect. His magic hadn't failed him but had given him a great reward. Two for one, and ugly mortal sisters at that.

The council's order had been clear. He wasn't to bring over any enchanted humans. Well, he wouldn't enchant the humans. He would enchant King Larus instead. Cupid chuckled and clapped his hands. He couldn't wait to see them fighting over the grand lycan king, chasing him about like he was a piece of meat.

Cupid's squat legs danced along the barren, over-grown bailey yard, kicking at the snow. His little arms pumped through the air. Two ugly mortals for the lycan king. Two ugly, discarded, unwanted mortals. They wouldn't be missed by the human world, not missed at all. He risked nothing in bringing them over, for no one would search for them. It was too perfect.

As the sisters walked back into the hall, Cupid was glad to be out of their hideous presence. Revenge was hard, repulsive work indeed. But if he repaid the lycan king, it would be well worth the torment.

He snickered in excitement, going to make his plan ready. As he turned to find the opening to his portal, his foot slipped in the snow and he landed hard on his backside. A howl of pain escaped him.

Ach. That was going to leave a mark.

4

"WHICH DIRECTION DO YOU THINK WE SHOULD GO?" Sophia asked, sipping at her stew. It was bland, made mostly of melted snow, but neither sister complained. They'd eaten much worse in the years since their father's death.

"You decide," Mina answered. Ever since she agreed to leave, a sense of melancholy had come over her. She didn't know if it was the right decision. She didn't know if she should change her mind.

"Winter will be harsh to the north, so mayhap the south? To France?" Sophia asked.

"To France then." Mina took a sip and nodded absently. Glancing at her sister, she asked, "Did you do something to the stew?"

Sophia shrugged. "No."

"It has an odd flavor to it."

"You made it." Sophia playfully wrinkled her nose. "So it's no wonder."

"I can cook well enough. It is you who nearly poisons us," Mina said, trying to draw her cloak around her shoulders. Even inside the castle it was chilly. It felt like ages since she'd been warm. She couldn't wait for the winter to end. "I'm cold. Would you put another log on the fire?"

"Sure, but we don't have that much firewood left." Sophia frowned. "Are you ill? You seem a bit pale."

"No, I-I am fine." Mina grabbed her head. She watched as Sophia's face swam before her eyes. She blinked slowly, feeling dizzy.

"Do you smell that?" Sophia stood to go to the fireplace. "It's wretched."

Sophia wobbled lightly on her feet before falling to her knees on the hard castle floor, never making it to the fireplace. A small sound escaped her throat as she swayed back and forth. Moaning, she fell over to the side.

"Sophia?" Mina demanded, struggling to stand. The world was spinning, and it was hard to move. The light-headedness became worse. She fought to stay awake as she tried to go to her sister.

"Sleep, sleep."

"What?" Mina began, looking around in search of

the shrill voice. Her vision stretched and bent at awkward angles. A horrible smell assaulted her senses, as she neared Sophia. She felt nauseous. Croaking, she demanded, "Who's there?"

"Such tired ladies, such ugly, tired ladies. Sleep, mortal, sleep."

"Show yourself, devil." Mina fell to her knees, her words lacking strength. Her limbs were numb, weak. Crawling forward, she tried to make it to her sister. Her fingers shook violently as she reached forward. Then, feeling the silk of blonde hair within her grasp, Mina moaned and collapsed on the stone floor, drifting into the blackness of sleep.

Cupid dropped the magical cloak and chuckled. Crossing to the two women on the floor, he grimaced as the soft glow of orange firelight caressed their smooth features. He waddled to the fireplace and dipped his fingers into the ashy soot. Swiping it over their flesh, he tried to hide their repulsiveness from view.

Once that was done he paused and looked about the crumbling hall. What a pity that two creatures such as these would get such a wonderful, beautiful home. He'd give anything to have the cold draft whistling through his cave.

Sighing, Cupid leaned over and grabbed the long length of their hair, not caring that he knocked their heads about as he worked. He quickly braided the horrible dark and light strands together to fashion a thick rope. Slinging the braid over his shoulder, he threw his hand up to open the portal back to his world. Then, bracing his legs, he grunted as he dragged the unconscious women behind him.

5

LARUS TOOK A DEEP BREATH, SIGHING AS HE LOOKED up into the red tree limbs of the forest. The wind whistled gently through the large pale leaves, quiet and peaceful. Twigs and forest debris littered the ground, giving his body warmth in the suddenly chilly air.

It felt as if snow might be coming. He wondered if the wizards were up to something. They rarely made snow since the realms had been separated. He yawned, unconcerned by it. His kind could well withstand the elements. After his long ordeal with the council, Larus needed this break—away from conflict and responsibility. He left Lycaon under Ilar's capable care, knowing the man would send for him if he were needed.

All around him, the forest was dense—too dense to see through. Little spots of light danced along the floor, shining through the high tree limbs. Being lycan, he didn't need his eyes to sense if anyone was around. He could easily smell or hear anything that came too near.

Rolling over on his stomach, he rested his tan, hairy chin on a paw and watched a trail of insects march past. His tail wrapped around his side and his leg twitched in contentment. Now this was the life, nature all around and no obligation in sight. His eyelids drooped lazily over his green wolfen eyes and he considered taking a nap right where he was.

Mina groaned, reaching for her head. Her tongue was thick in her mouth and her throat dry. She felt terrible as if horses had trampled her in her sleep. Her arms were weak and shaky when she lifted them. Without looking, she knew she was bruised and scraped along her back and legs. She opened her eyes, rolling them about in her head. Her vision blurred strangely. Tree limbs flashed before her, streaking like angry claws against the purple sky.

"Purple?" she mumbled. When she tried to sit up, her hair pulled and her head spun. She yelped in pain, falling back down to the ground with a heavy thud.

"Ah." Sophia screamed next to her in irritation.

"Sophia?" Mina asked, reaching to feel the top of her head as she tried to look to her side. Her sister lay next to her, blinking in confusion. Green eyes stared from a face covered in dark gray soot. Sophia's body jerked as if to sit up and they both again yelped as their hair was pulled.

"Mina, stop it." Sophia cried. Then, as she struggled for breath, she looked around the forest. Her round gaze turned back to stare into her sister's. "What's going on? Where are we? Why is the sky purple?"

"You see it too?" Mina asked, growing uneasy.

"Yes, but..." Sophia tried to sit up once more and they both were rewarded with a shock of pain to their tender scalps.

"Ow." They grunted in unison.

"Quit wiggling about, Sophia," Mina demanded in annoyance. "I think we're bound together."

Cupid paused behind a large tree in his progress across the forest. Poking his wrinkled head around the corner, he waited. King Larus was close. He could feel that the lycan was near. It was an easy enough tracking spell that he'd used to find the wolf king, and he knew he wouldn't be detected so long as the spell was in place. Otherwise,

Larus with his keen lycan senses would have discovered him immediately.

Bah. Accursed lycan.

Cupid's beady eyes searched the forest before making a run for another tree. It was slow going on his stubby legs, made more so by the fact that he limped from having fallen in the snow. Grunting, he came to a stop.

Cupid rubbed his back along the thick bark, wincing as it poked along his spine. He hated to let them go, but even he could admit that maybe it was time to put some salve on his back sores. They were almost too painful to tolerate. But, as his mother always said, beauty was pain and there was nary a creature prettier than a troll.

Suddenly, Cupid stopped and sniffed. His overlarge nose pointed up into the air. Ah, yes, King Larus was close indeed. Grinning, he pulled a hollow tube from his pocket and loaded it with a dart. Then, taking aim at the large tan wolf he found in the distance, he forced the giddy pleasure from his limbs so he could hit his target.

"Ah."

Cupid winced at the sound of the mortal's cry. Larus's head shot up from where he slept. It was now or never. Cupid blew, striking the lycan king in the hind leg. Larus growled. He whipped his head around. Cupid fumbled for a second dart and made ready to hit the wolf again.

"Ow." came a second cry.

Bah. Damn mortals. Too much noise. Too much.

The second sound drew Larus's attention. He lifted his head into the air and sniffed. Cupid panicked, trying to hurry. Larus took off in a sprint.

Cupid lifted his arm to aim and blew, his cheeks puffing at the effort. The dart flew long, striking a tree instead. The wolf was gone before he could try a third time.

"Bah." Cupid screeched in anger. He'd missed. With only one dart, only one mortal would fall in love with Larus—the first to lay eyes on him. The other would remain unaffected. This wasn't good. He saw his plans crumbling around him.

"Bah. Bah. Bah." Cupid jumped up and down in a great show of fury, waving his arms around his head like a madman. Then, still frustrated, he kicked the base of a tree. Stubbing his toe, he yelped in pain and fell over on the ground to cradle the injured foot.

"Stop moving. It's our hair," Mina said, finding the end of their waist-length locks tied together. It was awkward in their position to work the braids free, but she tried anyway. Whoever did it had done a horrible job of weaving them together.

All of a sudden, a snarl sounded. Mina froze. The locks fell from her trembling fingers.

"Sophia?" she asked. "Can you see? What is that?"

"Huh?" Sophia's voice was weak.

"Sophia, what growled?" Mina insisted, her heart hammering in her chest. A strange sensation worked over her limbs, and she felt as if they were being watched. She grabbed their hair and worked at a frantic pace, finally freeing the ends so she could begin to unwrap the knotted braid. "Can you find a weapon? Feel around."

"Huh?" Sophia repeated.

The growl sounded again and Mina stiffened in fear. A shadow fell across her face. She turned up to where a large tan wolf stood above her. By the breadth of his shoulders, she guessed him to be at least three times the size of any wolf she'd ever heard of. His massive paw lifted, reaching for her face. Mina whimpered. It was a weak sound in the back of her throat. Her breath came in strange pants.

She stayed focused on the paw. The wolf shook ever so slightly, his tan fur rippling all along his dangerous body. The paw near her face transformed into a human hand, strong, callused, very masculine. Soon the hairy arm was to follow, disappearing into dark muscular flesh. Her gaze followed the rippling effect of the transformation, as it moved to the creature's face. Only the eyes stayed the same startling dark green shade as human features filled in where the wolf's had been.

Mina still couldn't move. It was the most amazing thing she'd ever seen in her life. Surely, he must be a demon to perform such tricks or a sorcerer who made a pact with the devil. Her breath hitched in her throat. But, could the devil have such beautiful, honest eyes? She realized her limbs were not stiff out of fear, but because this man was the most handsome she'd ever seen. His face was hard, perfect, chiseled. A sweep of long, dark blond hair reached to her, tickling her neck. His mouth curled slightly in confusion, as he looked at her, so close to smiling, yet not quite.

That's when she noticed his shoulders were bare, as was his chest. Her heart fluttered, making a wave of pleasure course through her body, working over her from where his hair brushed the pulse at her neck. It warmed her blood and caused tingling in her stomach. Her eyelids felt heavy and she let them drop. Unbidden, Mina dropped her tangled hair and reached for him. She stared at his mouth, desperately wanting him to kiss her. Every nerve in her body begged him to touch her.

"I love you."

Mina frowned, turning to the side to glance at Sophia. Her sister's eyes were filled with the same haze Mina felt and she too reached for the man. Sophia had a daft, smitten smile on her dirty face as she moved boldly to touch him.

"I love you," Sophia said again, sighing dreamily. "I give all that I am to you, my lord. Let me love you."

Without an apparent thought in her head, Sophia sat up, moving as if she were under a spell. Mina flinched as their hair was yanked apart. Sophia didn't seem to notice.

The man frowned and backed away from Sophia's reach, crouching like an animal as he moved. Mina reached to stop her sister from mindlessly following him. Keeping a firm grip on Sophia's lax arm, she turned to glare at the strange creature.

He squatted before them, nude. Mina gasped, her words of irritation dying on her lips as she saw the full glory of his muscled body. His flesh was tanned, giving him a warm glow. Not an ounce of fat marred his frame from his broad shoulders to his narrowed waist. His head tilted to the side to study them.

Mina's mouth went dry. She had seen men before without clothes, but none such as him. His member lay limp next to his thigh, nestled in a bed of dark blond hair. As she stared, it twitched. She felt the blood rush from her head. She was no naive fool, though she'd never been with a man. As noblewomen, their purity was the one commodity they had, especially now that their father was dead, and they had no money and land to offer a husband as an enticement.

"*Mm.*" Sophia struggled to be free. She lifted her hand as if to touch the man's chest. Only Mina's hold stopped her. "Let me go. I wish to prove my love to my lord."

Mina shook herself back to reality. If Sophia felt the same way as she, it was undoubtedly a trick or a demonic spell. Her voice sharp, she demanded, "Who...? *What* exactly are you? And why have you brought us here?"

6

HUMANS.

Larus grimaced, eyeing the dirty-faced maidens. It just had to be humans. The scent of them was unmistakable. They were from the realm of mortals. His frown deepened. It would seem he'd never be free of their kind. They were spilling into his world like rodents.

Eyeing the light-haired one first, he felt the tiniest stirring inside him. She stared adoringly at him, licking her lips in open invitation. He was a man who knew well the look of seductive encouragement and the woman was beautiful to behold.

Larus moved to study the dark-haired woman. Her look was now the opposite of what it had been. She no longer looked pleased at his attention, though he thought to still smell her desire. If ever he imagined two temptresses, this would be what his mind created—two young, pretty sisters, matching in almost all ways but temperament.

At first, he thought them fairies or elves by the way they looked at him with obvious lust. Their pheromones were strong, calling to him. It was very rare that the delicate creatures would seek to attract a wolf, as lycan were known as wild lovers.

For a moment, when the humans were both staring at him, their eyes begging for kisses, he'd almost given in. It wouldn't be the first time he took two women to his bed, and these two would be lovely visions atop his excited body. But, there was more than just desire inside him. There was a stirring of bloodlust.

Some immortal women had a penchant for the beast so that wasn't so unusual. However, smelling the unmistakable mortal scent in the sisters, his desire died just as quickly as it grew. He wouldn't tempt the beast inside him. Fairies would heal, mortals would not.

The dark one's gaze bored into him with accusation, which fueled his blood even more. When Larus first saw her, a jolt of bold desire had struck through his system and he'd been sure she felt it too. He couldn't explain it, but he wished it were her stare that was dreamy. Her hostility only provoked the hunter in him, making the beast even more desperate to come out and play.

Deciding the dark one was the only one with her wits about her, Larus directed his questions to her. With ease he used the old tongue all immortals knew but rarely used. Thanks to Rhiannon's presence, he'd had time to practice it. Most elders made a point of remembering the old language, so if ever the mortals came back into their world, they would be prepared. "What are you doing in this realm, mortal? Your kind isn't welcomed here."

"Well, *nieten*," the dark one answered, sneering. "Obviously someone wanted us here or else we'd not be here."

Her eyes tried to drift down over his body and he was sure her cheeks turned a bright pink beneath the soot on her face. Her lush lips parted. They were lips he instantly wanted to feel on his body, kissing and sucking every inch of him. Larus frowned, following her glance down over his naked frame. With a growl, he ordered, "Don't move."

Standing, he stalked off into the trees. He wasn't worried. If they did run, he'd be able to hunt them down. No human could outrun a lycan.

He was unsure as to what annoyed him more. Was it the fact that he seemed to be surrounded by mortals? Or was it that the strongest rush of desire he'd felt in a very long time would be going unanswered?

It didn't take him long to find his clothes. Suddenly remembering the sting he'd gotten as he awakened from a deep sleep, he frowned. Insects usually didn't bother his kind. Larus looked at his leg and found a welt. His frown deepened. The welt had an odd pink ring around its edge.

"Great," he mumbled, grabbing the large rectangle of cloth that was his tunic. He swung it over his body, knotting it together at his shoulders with practiced ease. His legs were also left naked, covered only by his leather boots. His kind rarely bothered with pants, as they only got in the way when they shifted. As was the style, his arms and a shoulder were left bare.

Larus paused in his task as he heard a strange chattering noise. Instantly his eyes filled with green-gold and he stiffed the air. Turning, he saw a squirrel running in circles around a tree. He grabbed his cloak and moved for a closer look. Imbedded in the tree was a dart.

Larus frowned, leaning over to pull the dart from the bark. To his surprise, the squirrel didn't move away, but simply hugged his little arms to the tree and held it. Usually small woodland creatures would sense the predator in him and run. This creature only appeared to see the tree.

Ignoring the critter, he studied the dart. Something was very strange about all this. He thought of Cupid.

But, as he sniffed to detect the troll's foul odor, he only got the fresh scent of nature. No, if Cupid was near, he would have smelled him a mile off.

Larus had more to worry about than a dart. For all he knew pixie children shot him with it, daring each other to provoke the giant lycan. His biggest problem was the mortal women. Had they come through the portal when Cupid opened it to Lady Rhiannon? It seemed unlikely for he'd seen the confusion on their faces as they looked upon him, unless they'd been sleeping for many months.

Larus was sure Cupid wouldn't be stupid enough to defy the elders by opening the portals again, even if he was angry. The only thing that made sense was that Cupid had left the portal open the first time. A growl of outrage built in his throat. Why had no one thought to check it? Was Cupid so incompetent as to risk everything the immortals had built over the three centuries since they'd been away from the mortal kind?

Larus let loose a string of dark curses as he stood. In anger, he threw the dart, embedding it back in the tree. There would be time to worry about that later, for now he had to tend to the women. He would drag them back to the opened portal and shove them through it, if it was the last thing he ever did. And, if Cupid had left the portal open, he might shove the troll to the other realm as well, making sure to lock him forever on the other side.

7

Mina watched the strange man-beast disappear into the trees. Struggling to her feet, she wobbled slightly before grabbing Sophia's arm. She roughly jerked her sister to stand. Under her breath, she said, "Come on, Sophia. By all that is holy, like we would actually stay here to await the devil's return."

"But... but, he said to stay and wait for him," Sophia whispered, as she was forced to move. "Mina, stop pulling. I love him."

"I said run." Mina tugged her sister behind her, sliding her hand over Sophia's arm to grab her wrist. Sprinting through the forest, she ignored Sophia's protests and declarations of love. She didn't know what was wrong with her sister and now wasn't the time to stop and figure it out. Whatever that man-beast was, she was sure that the devil had something to do with him. Surely the best plan was to get away from him.

Mina's heart thundered in her chest, but not from their short sprint. She was terrified. The man-beast did something to them. She felt it, when she first looked into his incredible green eyes, so curious, so trusting, so deep and soulful. Something about him made her want to grab him close and declare her love for him. That something was surely a curse, a devil's curse. And, if he wasn't a devil, then he was surely the son of one. For who else could call forth the transformation into a hairy wolf-beast?

Mina's legs tangled in the skirt of her dirty gown as she tried to jump over a fallen log. She tripped, losing her hold on Sophia's hand. Instantly, Sophia turned and began marching back the way they had come, yelling, "I must obey my master, for without his happiness I am not whole. I need him, Mina."

Mina growled in frustration and rushed after her. Clutching Sophia firmly by the wrist, she yanked her sister from behind. Sophia made a weak noise, but her body had no fight in it and she unwillingly obeyed as she was once again dragged forward.

"Sophia, he is a *nieten*. A man-beast. Please, come on. Hurry," Mina begged. She heard the rustling of leaves behind them and knew the creature followed close. Part of her was torn, wanting to stop so he might catch them. She ignored that part of her, damning it for a fool.

"I don't care what he is. He is my *nieten*," Sophia announced as stubborn as a child. "I love him. I want to be with him and nothing you can say will stop us. You hate him. You just don't want us to be together. You want him for yourself."

"Blessed saints, are you mad? Sophia, listen to yourself. Why would I want him if I hate him?" Seeing a cave, Mina tugged her sister up the small incline and into the opening. "Now, hurry. Please."

Sophia whimpered in protest. Mina didn't care. She pulled her sister into the dark cave and wrapped her hand over her mouth. Holding her close, she hugged Sophia tightly to her chest. She bit her lip, listening to the creature run past them. Even after the sound of his footfalls had faded, she didn't relax her guard.

Tears of worry came to Mina's eyes. There was something terribly wrong. Sophia wasn't acting like herself. Her sister would never fall in love so easily. She highly doubted her sister would ever fall in love. Whatever sorcerer's spell the *nieten* put on Sophia, it was a horrible curse. It could only mean his intentions toward them were dark in purpose.

"Oh, what fools these mortal be, coming into this cave without an invitation."

Mina gasped and even Sophia stopped her weak struggles at the sound. Slowly, their heads turned to look into the den. Just enough light fell onto the creature who spoke to make out the hideous array of sharp, pointed teeth. If not for the voice, they'd have mistaken it for a wild animal.

Mina's hand slipped from her sister's mouth. Sophia screamed. The creature reared its ugly face and screamed back—louder and high pitched. Both sisters jolted at once, falling from the cave's opening and rolling down the small incline to the forest floor.

Almost immediately, the *nieten* was back, still in the form of a human but now dressed. His long green cloak flowed as he ran toward them. With a deft twist of his fingers, the material slid off his arms to the ground. Beneath the cloak, he was indecently clad in only a draping tunic that fell to the top of the knees.

"Oh," Sophia sighed from her place on the ground, sounding very much like a witless maid. "My lord. You found us. I knew you would. I told Mina not to run away from you. You must forgive her. She can be quite ridiculous."

Mina looked around and picked up a nearby branch. Standing, she wielded it before her like a sword. She turned first to the *nieten* and then to the frightful crea-ture covered in fine black fur from head to foot, and yelled, "Stay back, both of you."

The black creature stood upright, though only as high as Mina's knee. More afraid of its sharp teeth than the man, she pointed the stick at it in warning. The crea-ture grinned, an awful expression of pleasure, and said, "Be they yours, lycan? They smell sweet and unclaimed. Run along and let me play with them, beast."

"I'm no man's or beast's." Mina proclaimed hotly.

"Yes," Sophia simpered. Mina blinked to see her sister drifting over to the half-naked man. Her arms lifted up to him. "I belong to him, heart and soul and body."

"Sophia." Mina commanded, gritting her teeth. She lunged to grab her sister's hair and missed. Her legs tangled in her skirt and she fell over.

"Yes, Uldra, they are mine." The man-beast reached over and pulled Sophia to him.

Mina looked up into the dark, penetrating gaze of the man. Her breath caught at the possessiveness of the man-beast's statement. A fire burned inside him, glinting hotly from his rigid features. He was furious.

His eyes stayed fixed on her, as he artfully swirled Sophia around, only to pull her back into his chest. Hot jealousy surged through Mina and she wanted to rip her sister from his arms. She shook violently and had the insane urge to hit the man over the side of the head with the stick—and not just because she wanted to free her sister.

The man's mouth twitched at the corner and she wondered if he could sense the jealousy in her. Mina forced all emotion from her face. Sophia sighed and nestled against his hold, content to be there. Her eyes drifted closed, as if her position was the most natural in the world. Envy nearly choked Mina as she watched.

"The creatures sleep and must not be disturbed. Only I may enter to feed them. Your women encroach." Uldra pointed his hairy little finger at the two humans in turn.

"My apologies, Uldra, they are simpleminded. I shall lead them away forthwith." The *nieten* kept his eyes trained on Mina in warning. She shivered, instinctively not saying a word.

"See that you do," Uldra said. He turned and with agile grace, leapt back up into the cave. Grumbling under his breath, he said, "I don't know why the council would let humankind back in. I think it's a fool's mistake. No good ever came from having a human around, unless it is to feed them to dragons."

"You are so brave, my handsome lord," Sophia gushed. She trailed her hand over the man's forearm,

And so strong. Have you a name,
.ght?"

," he answered, distracted. He stared at
.ade it a point to glare back. "Come, we have
of here. Uldra is a testy character and you don't
o wake the beasts he tends."

"I am Lady Sophia of Aucester and this is my sister, Lady Willamina." Sophia continued to stroke Larus's arm. Sighing, she turned her cheek into his chest and began to rub against him.

"Let her go," Mina demanded, taking a shaky breath. Anger, raw and hot, took over her body. She had just about had enough of this man and his domineering manners. Slowly, she got to her feet, pulling the stick up behind her back. "Sophia, come away from him this instant."

"Why, dear sister? He is my heart. Without him I'm not whole." Sophia rubbed her back into his side, trying to entice him to look at her. He kept his eyes fixed on Mina.

Sophia lifted her hand to his jaw and pulled his face to force him to look at her. Larus frowned and instantly let her go, putting her away from him. The moment her sister was out of harm's way, Mina took the opportunity to swing for Larus's head. His hand shot out with lightning speed and stopped the attack. The stick smacked his

palm. He didn't even flinch and his eyes never
away as he continued to stare at her.

"If you will not obey, I will take you by force," La
said, not once looking at the stick they both held. For
moment, their eyes warred in a silent battle. His har
gaze swirled with liquid amber. Her fingers shook, and
she was the first to let go. The man-beast tossed the stick
aside, and it landed with a hard swish in a nearby shrub.

Before Mina knew what was happening, she was
held flush to a muscled chest and captured in a vice-like
grip. A steady heart beat beneath her cheek. The soft
material of his green tunic pressed into her face and
neck, warmed from his body. It had been a long time
since she felt such warmth. The press of flesh molded
against her, as hard as stone and as smooth as polished
marble. Hair tickled her forehead, and she wasn't sure if
it was hers or his. Shivers wracked her length.

The sheer power of his touch took her by surprise,
and she didn't protest as much as she should have. Whatever he was, he felt good against her. The subtle smell of
the forest surrounded her, tinged by the natural scent of
man. It teased her senses, numbing her thoughts. In a
moment of insanity, she liked the feel of him holding her.
She felt safe and protected by his nearness.

Her body stirred, becoming warm in unfamiliar
ways. Men had attracted her in the past, but not such as

this. The attraction scared her, for she didn't wish to become witless like Sophia.

"Mina." Sophia yelled, her voice full of venom. "What do you think you are doing? Get off him. He is my knight. He is mine. Mine. Mine. Mi—"

"Sophia," Larus said firmly, in a low voice that gave both women obvious chills. Mina tried to lift her head to look more fully at her sister, but he held her face to his chest. Sophia stood in mid-stride, her mouth hanging open as she waited for the man to speak. "Gather my cloak for me."

Sophia's expression instantly changed from anger to smitten adoration. She nodded happily and went to get the cloak from the ground. She dusted it off before handing it to him. Mina watched all this speechless, feeling betrayed and alone.

When Larus reached for the cloak, Mina jerked herself free and tried to get away. She made it two steps before the man growled and tackled her from behind. Landing on the ground with a thud, she felt his heavy length down her spine, crushing the breath from her lungs. With an angry pull, he hauled her around to face him. Straddling her with his thighs, he pinned her arms above her head with one hand.

Helpless and trapped, Mina struggled to be free, whimpering softly. But she only succeeded in forcing him against her smaller frame in hard jolts, tightening his hold over her. The intimate stroke of his body rubbed indecently against her core, heating her sex and making her very aware of him. She breathed deeply, unsure of what to do next.

Larus gave her a wicked look. His gaze raked hotly over her breasts. Mina tried to shake loose, terrified by how that look made her skin tingle with the longing to be touched by him.

With a few deft movements, he had her wrapped up and tied in the large cloak. Her head poked out of the top, her feet out the bottom. She struggled, wiggling around on the ground like a worm. The man stood above her, hands on hips, as he watched her sputtering and cursing beneath him. He waited until she was breathless, huffing for air, her energy spent.

"Speak and I will gag you," he warned. Leaning over, he hauled Mina over his broad shoulder and turned to look at Sophia. His hands settled indecently along the back of Mina's thigh, close to the bottom curve of her butt cheek. "Come, we need to get away from this cave before we anger those within. We'll camp tonight. I will decide what to do with you two on the morrow."

"I'll tell you what you can do, yo—" Mina began, trying to knee him in the chest in her precarious position. She never finished. Larus whipped her off his shoulder.

Screaming she writhed as she became air-bound, falling toward the earth. She never hit. He caught her in his arms before gently lowering her to the ground. She glared at him, but it did little to stop his intent. Within seconds he had her gagged.

"I warned you," he said simply, tossing her wiggling form over his shoulder once more. He gripped her tightly in his arms, holding her around the upper thighs. She felt his touch all the way to her curling toes. "Though, I am somehow not surprised you didn't listen."

Cupid looked down from his high perch in vast amusement. He still wasn't happy about missing Larus with the dart, but things were turning out fine. The dark-haired human was feisty. He liked that, though she was still as ugly as a patch of flowers. She would give Larus plenty of grief. Besides, it was vastly amusing to see her bound in such a way.

The blonde human upset him some. She batted her hideous lashes and pursed her lips, but she had yet to throw her body onto Larus's. She had yet to kiss the lycan king. Cupid shivered, knowing that even his stout stomach couldn't handle seeing that show. Just the thought made him nauseous. Her firm lips, so full, so red, so bowed, pressed to Larus's lycan mouth, flicking her horribly pink tongue between his lips.

Cupid moaned, grabbing his stomach. He swayed on his branch. His face drained of color as he felt bile burning in the back of his throat. The mere thought was too much. He couldn't take it. He was going to...

Cupid gagged so hard, he retched violently down the tree's side. He grabbed at the bark, trying to keep the world from swaying beneath him. Watching his meal fall to the ground, he hissed in anger. It had taken him a good week to decay that squirrel. Now what was he going to eat? It was hard to find rotted animals in the forest that weren't picked apart by scavengers.

Irritable, he kicked the tree. Cupid yelped in surprise as pain shot through his already injured ankle. He lost hold of the branch and fell over, tumbling his way to the hard ground.

8

Larus kept a fast pace as he made his way through the forest. Now that the dark one was quiet, he could think. Out of his lycan form, he was about a week away from Lycaon. He wasn't sure if he should take the mortal women back to his home, or if he even wanted to, but he didn't know what else to do with them.

He thought about taking them to Fenris, to Lord Malak's keep. There was a portal near there, though not the one the troll would have used. Or, perhaps, he should take them before the elders. As soon as he thought it, Larus knew he should probably do that. The elders would fight over what to do with them, more than likely decide to seal the portals and keep the two women trapped in the magic realm. It was possible they'd make the women Larus's permanent wards. He would be honor bound to care for them. With the dark one's nearness already tormenting him, it wasn't a prospect he relished.

As they walked, the blonde next to him made soft sounds, trying to draw his attention. He sighed in frustration and looked at her, wondering if she was simpleminded or simply under a spell. She smiled brightly at his attention and he nearly flinched at her insipid look.

Mina had stopped trying to kick him and now rested over his shoulder. He much preferred her to fight him. For, when she didn't move, he had much time to contemplate the smell of her body, namely the part between her thighs, which was dangerously close to his head. The perfume made his mouth water to taste her until he could practically feel her intimately against his tongue. Her backside was soft and womanly beneath his hand, making it hard not to caress her. A few times he purposefully stepped in a shallow hole, he had an excuse to bounce his hand along her flesh. He'd forgotten how soft human bodies could be, how fragile compared to the steel muscles of his kind. Even lycan women were physically tough. The dominant hunter in him liked that softness very much.

"Sophia," he said. "We will make camp here. Gather wood for a fire and stay close."

"Yes, Larus," she said, sighing prettily. She twirled a

strand of her blonde hair between her fingers. On his shoulder, Mina grunted.

"Call for me if you run into trouble." Larus stiffly nodded at her. He couldn't keep his eyes from dipping down over her young body. She looked as soft as her sister. Then why did his body want one and not the other? Maybe he was a glutton for torture, picking the ill-tempered over the fair. Though, he knew the hunter in him stirred to Mina. As badly as he wanted to claim her body, his mouth wanted to drink her blood. It was dangerous that he should feel such an impulse after so long.

Larus set Mina on the ground to look her over. She felt light in his arms, thin. When he let go, she swayed to the side, appearing close to fainting. He caught her up, holding her closer than he should have. She blinked in confusion only to glare up at him, every bit as angry as when he tied her up. He grinned, unable to help it. This woman had a lot of spirit.

"Do you promise to behave?" he asked. She vehemently shook her head in denial. He licked his lips, pleased to see her eyes following his tongue. Why was he torturing himself? He didn't want her as his lover. Well, his body did want her, but his mind was stronger and it told him to dump her in the forest and run for the hills. His voice lowered a timbre, to a seductive rumble that had melted many stubborn women. "Very well. I have no wish to keep you tied, but it appears as if you enjoy it. Let me know what else you enjoy, my lady, and I'll do my best to please you."

Why did he just say that? He hadn't meant to. What was it about her?

He didn't think it possible, but her big eyes widened. Larus reached for her and took the gag from her mouth. Mina flexed her jaw and continued to glare hotly.

"Hate me as you wish, Lady Willamina," Larus stated, pretending to be unconcerned. "But the gag was for your protection. Had you continued to yell and wake the dragons, we would have had to fight them off. They are ill-tempered when their sleep is disrupted and would have eaten you for sure. I might have been tempted to let them."

"What did you do to my sister?" Mina demanded vehemently, ignoring his threat.

Larus looked at her in confusion. His hands were still on her body and it was distracting his train of thought. Heat unfurled in his stomach, hardening his shaft with molten desire. He shifted uncomfortably at her expectant look. "Did you not hear? I sent her for firewood."

"Not that," she snapped. "You know what I mean."

"My heart." Sophia called, coming toward him. "Will this do, my love? Or shall I gather you more?"

Larus looked uncomfortable. He forced Mina to the ground, helping her so she wouldn't fall. Without really looking, he mumbled, "Uh, yes, that is fine."

He took the limbs from Sophia and moved away from both sisters to build a fire. Keeping his back turned, he concentrated on pushing the blood from his lower extremities, back into his brain. As he lit the flame, he heard Sophia behind him saying softly, "No, I can't release you, Mina. My lord tied you up and I will not go against him."

Mina grunted in response and he hid his small grin. She was persistent. He'd give her that. Dusting off his hands, he looked from one woman to the other. "Stay here, Sophia. I go to hunt our dinner."

Out of habit, he unknotted the tunic at his shoulder as he walked so that he could shift to better track their food. Hearing a small gasp behind him as the tunic dropped off his shoulders to hang around his waist, he stiffened. Larus decided it was best to undress in the forest out of the blonde one's view. Already her eyes were a little starry when she looked at him.

MINA CURSED HERSELF FOR GASPING AT LARUS'S naked back. Luckily, Sophia had been too busy staring to notice her reaction to it. She knew he heard the sound, had seen it in the subtle shift of his weight when he moved. Let him think it was Sophia. Her sister was already making a fool of herself.

"Sophia." Mina demanded for the third time in a row. The woman wasn't hearing her. "Sophia, untie me now or I will never forgive you."

Sophia blinked, looking hurt. "It's not my fault you can't behave, Mina. Besides, I told you I couldn't untie you. My sweet Larus doesn't wish it and I live only to please him."

Mina felt anger rolling in her chest. She was tired, hungry, and so damned frustrated she wanted to hit something—anything. Her legs were stiff but had finally stopped tingling as they went blessedly numb from lack of movement. Forcing a calm breath, she tried to reason, "Sophia, listen to me. I love you. You're my sister, my blood, and I love you. Now please. I promise to be good. Untie me."

Sophia's features softened as she looked at her sister. A smile crept to her lips. Her arms reached forward.

Finally. Mina thought.

"Oh, Mina," Sophia said, throwing her arms over Mina's bound body. "That's so sweet of you to say. I love you, too. And it does my heart good to know you approve of my Larus. For I will tell you a secret," leaning to her sister's ear, she whispered, "I plan to marry him."

Mina flinched as Sophia planted a kiss on her cheek. When her sister pulled away, she still wasn't free. Mina made a weak sound of complete frustration.

"But I still can't untie you." Sophia turned back to the fire. "Not until my love says I may. I live for him now, only and always for him."

They sat in silence for a long while. Mina cursed Larus and her sister, nearly succeeding in convincing herself that she didn't care anymore if he kept Sophia all to himself. Let them have each other.

Hearing a rustling, both sisters stiffened. Larus came out of the forest, fully dressed. In one hand he carried two skinned rabbits. In the other he held a torn piece of wet cloth.

"Wash the soot from your face," he said, tossing it to Sophia. "And cleanse your sister as well."

Sophia obeyed. Larus watched them guardedly, giving nothing away. Mina grumbled, struggled some, but in the end let her sister clean her face.

"Can you prepare these?" he asked Sophia when she'd finished, lifting the rabbits.

Mina snorted. "She can barely put two spices together."

Sophia made a weak noise, looking wounded. Larus frowned. He seemed to be considering asking Mina for a moment, but then finally began doing it himself. Mina was glad. If he thought she was going to cook for him, he was sorely mistaken.

"Here."

Mina blinked, looking up in surprise. Larus stared down at her. His eyes narrowed as he held food out for her to take. She arched a brow, lifting her hands against her cloak prison before letting them drop. The smell of roasted meat assaulted her and her mouth watered.

"Are you going to behave so that I may untie you?" Larus asked.

Forcing herself to look away from the meat, she said, "I'm not hungry.

"By all the lycan," he grumbled, mumbling something in a language she couldn't understand. Thrusting the meat at Sophia, he ordered, "Hold this."

Sophia instantly obeyed, sighing softly at him in complete adoration.

"I should just let you starve," Larus said. He untied her, jerking roughly at the binds. Within seconds, he had her free, standing before him. "But you look as if you are already halfway there."

Mina moved to stretch her legs, wobbling, but too proud to fall over as she felt the prickling of returning blood to her limbs. Larus took the meat from Sophia and again held it out to her. He motioned gently for her to take it. "Here, eat."

Mina wanted to take it, but she couldn't. "I don't eat things that have been in a mongrel's mouth."

Larus's jaw fell momentarily slack in disbelief at her words. Sophia gasped. Mina's stomach chose that moment to growl loudly in hunger. His lips twitched into a mocking smile.

"Oh, she didn't mean that." Sophia said. Then, hastily, she added in an oddly cheerful voice, "That's not true, Mina. Remember that horrible black dog Sir Richard kept before he abandoned us like the others?"

Mina paled, looking at Sophia in horror. She wasn't going to tell him about *that*, was she? Her sister didn't even seem to be paying attention to her words as she picked at her food and ate. Sophia grinned happily. Mina felt as if she might retch at any moment.

"Yes, it broke into the larder and was eating our last piece of venison. That meat was in a mongrel's mouth and we ate it that very night. Remember, you killed the dog with a sword." Sophia continued to pick at her food, glancing up at Larus and then her sister. "In fact, didn't we even eat the dog?"

"No." Mina grabbed her temple, feeling dizzy after that horrible tale. She'd been covered in the dog's blood—an animal she'd played with several times before everything changed and the animal had become a wild, hungry beast. The last thing she wanted at the moment was to remember all they'd done to survive the last couple of years. "We gave it to the peasants to feed their children."

"Ah, yes, I remember now," Sophia said.

Larus's gaze was still fixed on Mina, challenging her as she glanced up at him. "I'm taking my sister and we are going, *nieten*. Thank you for the meal, and for protecting us from dragons, but we must be on our way."

"Lycan," he stated.

"What?" Mina asked, confused. "Liken to what?"

"My kind," Larus said through tight lips, "are called *lycans*. Not beast or man-beast or *nieten*. Say it. Lycan."

"No," Mina answered defiantly. She pressed her lips together as she shook her head in firm denial.

"Lycans," Sophia giggled. "I like that. It's lovely. Lycans. I like the lycan."

Mina glared at her sister. Larus's hand shot out and

gripped her jaw, forcing her face back to him. She gasped in surprise, feeling the shock of him through her entire being.

"Say it," he said, his tone low, "for I'll not ask you again."

Mina contemplated keeping her mouth shut, but his grip only tightened on her jaw, prying her lips apart. Her tone low, she said bitterly, "Lycan."

"Very good, my lady," Larus said, his voice dipping to that soft, seductive timbre. He didn't let her go, keeping her eyes forced on his. "Now, you and your sister aren't going anywhere. I found you so you are my responsibility until I can figure out how you got here in the first place. Then I will try to get you home."

"We are not your concern, and I don't see how our being here is yours to figure out," Mina said. "And we'll take our chances in the forest. I think we are safer there than with you."

"My lady," he said, pulling her face closer to his as he spoke. He kept his hand firm on her jaw. "If you think I am the most dangerous thing in the realm, you are sorely mistaken. Right now it's light, but during the dark the vampires come out to play."

Mina's face was blank.

"Have you not heard of them? They're vicious creatures with sharp teeth and handsome faces. One look into their eyes and you will be drawn forward to their deadly embrace." Larus drew closer still until his breath tickled her skin. She stood transfixed by him and it seemed to Mina that he had that power to entrance, that he spoke of himself and his eyes. His lids lowered over his steamy gaze, a gaze that was suddenly soft and inviting. Whispering, he continued, "One kiss and they'll drain you of every drop of blood in your fragile human body."

"What is going on?" Sophia asked, rising to her feet. She looked at Larus and then suspiciously to Mina. "Mina. What are you doing?"

"Eat, my lady, before this mongrel's mouth tears you apart," Larus threatened, pushing Mina away from him.

Mina saw the glint of fire in his eyes and hurriedly took the food from his hand. He stared her down and she quickly bit into it, taking a dainty, ladylike bite. It was good, lightly flavored. But, most importantly, it was food. Larus nodded at her in grim approval and turned his back. When he wasn't looking, she nearly devoured the meal, tearing off large chunks and swallowing them whole.

Sophia eyed her suspiciously a moment longer before sitting back on the log.

"You are a wonderful cook," Sophia said to Larus.

Abruptly, Mina stopped eating, feeling a little sick.

She looked down at Sophia. Her brown eyes were cloudy as she stared at Larus's backside. That wasn't her sister. It couldn't be. This world was playing tricks on her. Her mind was playing tricks. In a rush everything hit her— lycans, Uldra, dragons, vampires. It couldn't be true. This was a nightmare. That had to be it. Men didn't change into wolves. The sky didn't hold such a purple hue. Trees were not reddish and leaves were not large and pale. Her sister didn't simper and act subservient to a man. The meat churned in her stomach.

This was a nightmare, her nightmare, and she was going to walk away. Handing the rabbit to the creature that looked like her sister, Mina turned to the forest. At the moment, she didn't care what was out in the trees. She planned to start walking until she fell over dead or she simply woke up.

"Mina?" Sophia's sweet voice called. But she knew that couldn't be her. Sophia would never bow to man. She loved her freedom too much. "Mina, where are you going?"

LARUS WASN'T SURE IF HE WANTED TO STRANGLE Mina or kiss her. Hell, he wasn't sure if he wanted to strangle or kiss Sophia. Mina fueled his desire to boiling and no doubt Sophia would willingly release him of it. What had happened to his self-possessed sanity?

No, they were humans. He couldn't, *wouldn't* do anything with them. He didn't want to, not really. Then why was his treacherous body nearly bursting to claim one of them?

"Mina?" Sophia's sweet voice called behind him. He cringed slightly, knowing he didn't want to take the light sister to his bed. She was already doe-eyed when she looked at him. His kind liked a challenge and Sophia wasn't even close. "Mina, where are you going?"

Larus blinked, frowning as he turned around. He

caught a glimpse of dark hair as Mina disappeared into the forest. Sighing, he moved to go after her, ordering Sophia, "Stay here."

"But," she gasped, and he ignored her.

Stalking into the forest, he picked up Mina's scent. She walked fast, but he caught up to her without breaking stride. "Lady Willamina, halt. I told you the forest is not safe."

She didn't seem to hear him, just kept walking. Jogging forward, he grabbed her arm and spun her around to face him. Her brown eyes tore at him. Now that the soot was gone from her, she looked even more beautiful. His stomach knotted. He couldn't move.

"You're not real," she said. "This isn't real."

Larus frowned at that. She was dazed, sad, lost. Her tormented look called out to him, begging him silently to make it better, to make it all go away.

"That's not my sister," Mina said. "You're not real."

Larus couldn't take it. A low growl sounded in the back of his throat. He shot forward, catching her face in his warm palm. She was chilled, shivering. He wondered if it was his touch that did it. The forest didn't feel cold.

"Such things as you do not exist," Mina said, obviously not convinced by his nearness. "This is a dream, a nightmare. None of it is real. I could fall off a cliff and it wouldn't matter."

Larus could sense that she didn't believe her own words. She was a strong woman, brave. She'd proven her loyalty to her sister. Without thought, he pulled her to his chest, saying softly, "It's real. I'm real."

She gasped as his lips met hers. He tried to hold back, tried not to kiss her, but it was of no use. Larus knew from that first moment he looked into her eyes that he would kiss her. When she didn't scream, didn't fight, he pushed her back into a tree, his body trapping her to him. He forced the beast inside him to go slow, not wanting to scare her.

Mina moaned, feeling as if she was being dragged out of a fog into the mist. Larus's mouth was warm, moving softly against her. She wouldn't have expected his kiss to be so soft, so tender and sweet. She felt the hard press of bark on her back, the roughness of it contrasting the smooth hot flesh against her front. Her lips parted as his tongue slid along the crease of her mouth. He took the offered parting and thrust in, just to the barrier of her teeth. A shock went through her, stirring her blood like never before. His words echoed in her head, making her dizzy.

It's real. I'm real.

He felt real, and she knew that it couldn't be a dream. She lifted her hand, pulled to touch him by a power outside herself. Mina needed to feel his realness, his solid heat. Gliding her hands hesitatingly up his arms to rest on his naked shoulders, she let him kiss her. Part of her soared that he would pick her over the preening Sophia, but it was a shallow victory, one she wouldn't dwell on.

Mina knew she should scream, try to get away, but she didn't want to. It had been a long time since she'd felt protection in any form. His lips moved along hers and they felt so good. Her stomach was tight with his nearness, and she instinctively knew that when he took the security of his body away, she'd be left feeling empty. She was tired of feeling empty. She wanted the completeness she felt next to him.

Larus's eyes were dark green and gold when he pulled back to look at her, devouring her with his fervent expression. His hands worked, clenching and unclenching softly along her neck. With slow purpose, he drew his fingers down her throat to the top of her chest. When she didn't move, only stared up into his hot gaze, a small smile curled his lips. He closed his eyes and drew forward once more.

Mina gasped as his mouth pressed harder. The first kiss had been a test and was nothing like the fiery explosion that now assaulted her senses. His tongue worked expertly to pry apart her mouth. His teeth nipped until she gasped. When her lips parted, he thrust his tongue boldly inside, groaning as he conquered her silken depths.

Mina grew dizzy and turned her head away to gasp for breath. Her heart pounded so loudly she heard nothing else. Larus didn't stop. His mouth only moved with her, trailing wet kisses from the corner of her lips to her throat, to lick and nibble at her ear. She panted for breath, stiffening in wonder as his hands boldly slid off her upper chest to cup her breasts fully in his palms.

Larus moaned. His body pressed harder into hers and she felt his stiffened rod pushing into her softer belly. It was fire to her skin and so very big. She knew what he wanted from her, though she'd never done it herself. Fear worked its way through her. Her eyes widened at the feel of his hips rocking into her. Pushing his shoulders lightly, she managed a weak gasp of protest. "No."

Instantly, Larus left her, taking his ravishing lips away. Her mouth was full, swollen with the heat of his kiss. He gripped her arms as he held her before him, keeping her distanced from his body. Mina swallowed nervously, not sure what to do. She waited for him to speak, to act.

"It would seem, my lady," Larus said, his face becoming an unreadable mask, "that this mongrel's mouth is good enough to kiss you."

Mina opened her mouth to speak, appalled by his words. Anger rekindled itself in her chest, but Sophia's jealous yell stopped her from screeching at him.

"Mina!"

Mina stiffened. Larus let her go, taking a step back.

"My love? Where are you? What are you doing?" This time Sophia's voice was soft, loving.

Mina shook her head, trying to rid herself of all lingering feelings. This man-beast wasn't safe. He was a demon. He had to be. There was no other reasoning for it. Perhaps this was her afterlife. Maybe they died in the cold, withered, crumbling hall of their childhood home. Or, possibly this was real, and he was trying to cast his spell over her as well. Swallowing, she asked, "What spell have you put on my sister, you demon?"

His features darkened at the insult.

"What do you want from us? Hasn't your master taken enough from us? Must he also take our sanity?" Mina didn't believe what she was saying, but the words were making Larus mad so she shouted them anyway. "Go to your master the devil and tell him to leave us alone. He has our home and our wealth and our family honor. He has our father."

Mina didn't wait for him to speak. By the dangerous, hard glint in his eyes, she doubted he could. Regretting her hot words almost instantly, she backed away from him. He followed her with his eyes and only the heavy rise and fall of his chest showed movement in his still body. When she was far away from him, she turned and ran back to the campsite, back to her awaiting sister.

"Where were you?" Sophia demanded, suspiciously eyeing her from head to toe. "Why are you flushed?"

"I fell," Mina lied, too rampant with emotion to feel guilty. "I went to relieve myself and your knight scared me."

"Oh," Sophia said, coming to her side. She placed her hands tenderly on Mina's shoulders. "Well you should have listened to my dear knight. He told you not to go to the forest. There are frightful beasts out there that could attack you."

Mina grimaced and pushed Sophia's hands from her arms. She thought of Larus, the sensation of his kiss still hot on her mouth. Under her breath, she grumbled, "Indeed."

Cupid shivered, spitting on the ground. His long lips trembled in disgust. It was horrible. He was going to have to stick hot pokers in his eyes to get the hideous image of Larus kissing the dark-haired one out of his head. Good thing his eyes would grow back. Good thing the lycan king had stopped when he did so Cupid could get away.

Ach. Bah. Ach.

It would be best if he left them alone for a while. Aye, he didn't want to be near if they tried that again. Cupid turned, walking away from them. It would be night soon anyway and then the beasts would come out to play. He didn't wish to run into them.

Give the dart time, time indeed. It might work to his advantage. If Larus kissed the dark one, then the affected light one would be jealous. As the magic's power grew, so would Lady Sophia's love for the lycan king, and so would her jealousy over him.

Cupid stuck his finger up his nose and thoughtfully dug around. Aye. Things were working out better than he could have ever hoped. He just didn't want to stay around to watch it unfold—at least not until the fighting started.

Mina was sore from sleeping on the ground. Not that a hard bed bothered her. She'd gotten used to such after they had burned their straw mattresses for kindling. It was the fact that Larus tied her hands and feet for the night that made her ache. He almost looked sorry as he did it, but he didn't say anything beyond the fact that he didn't trust her to stay put for the night, and he didn't feel like saving her should she attract unwanted attention to herself.

It wasn't necessary. Despite any of the heatedly brave words she'd shouted at him, she was terrified of the forest. After her food settled, and she felt more like her old self, she thought long and hard about seeing Larus shift from his wolf form and the strange keeper of dragons, Uldra. She was sure she didn't want to run across anything more terrifying than those two. Besides, she'd never leave Sophia. The day before when she walked off had been a moment of insanity. She would have turned back eventually, Mina was sure of it.

Sophia had tried to sleep next to Larus. Mina felt an enormous sense of relief when he denied Sophia's obvious advances and ordered that she stay beside her sister—on the other side of the fire from him. Mina told herself that her relief was because she was worried about Sophia, but in truth she knew it was something much pettier than that. Ever since Larus had kissed her, she felt more possessive of him. Every time her sister looked at him, she wanted to scratch Sophia's eyes out.

Just thinking about the kiss made blood rush to her cheeks. As if sensing her sudden discomfort, Larus glanced back at her. She stiffened, trying to pass her red cheeks off as anger. His green eyes swirled with an amber light before he turned forward once more.

Looking ahead, Mina watched as Sophia tried to walk close to Larus. Her sister wore his green cloak about her shoulders, hugging the extra length in her arms. Larus sighed, moving over slightly until he was again on the edge of the path. Several times he was obliged to push Sophia away, back onto her side. He said nothing and ignored her sister's hurt, pouting expressions.

Mina wasn't sure where they were going or why she

so willingly followed behind them. When she asked, he merely told her they were going someplace safer than the forest. She wasn't sure she trusted their lycan companion, but so far he'd done them no real harm—not counting tying her up, hauling her about, and the ache in her belly each time he touched her.

Fine. She shouldn't trust him but it's not like they had any other knights coming forward to help them.

As Sophia's hand boldly tried to capture his, Larus jerked. Stopping, he looked down at her. His face was tight and Mina wondered if he was going to lose his temper. Her sister batted her eyelashes at him as he took a deep, ragged breath. It was clear he fought for control.

"By all the lycan, Sophia, go... pick flowers," Larus ordered her, biting back his irritation. "Now."

Sophia grinned and ran off to obey. Larus watched her for a moment in silence. Then, turning to Mina, he asked in exasperation, "What is wrong with her? Was she born touched in the head? I know it has not always been in human nature to take care of people like that, not like we immortals do. It's good to see things have changed in the last three hundred years and that you now take care of your own, but can't you control her—"

"Sophia is not touched." Mina interrupted his obvious irritation. "One of your kind did this to her. She was fine until we awoke here."

"Lycans wouldn't do such a thing. We lack the magic," Larus said matter-of-factly.

"Wait, did you just try to tell me you're immortal and over three hundred years old?" Mina asked. He hadn't moved closer to her, but she felt as if he was right next to her. His eyes bore steadily into hers, not turning away, and she couldn't help but feel his kiss anew upon her lips. She felt ashamed of her dirty old gown and her messy, wild hair. Why would he even want to kiss her? "Why are you staring? It's rude to stare. How can you lack magic? I saw you change. You have to be well versed in the black arts."

Larus grinned. "Perchance it's you who is touched, Lady Willamina? You don't seem to be following a single thought very well. Why is that?"

Mina gasped. It took her a while to realize he only teased her. His eyes sparkled with mischief and she couldn't help but blush. Larus's head tilted to the side, and he took a step toward her.

His voice lowered, and he leaned into her. "I am immortal and well over three hundred years of age, and though there are ways I can die, it will not be by the hand of time. My shifting into lycan form and back again is as natural as the sunset and isn't considered magical. It is as natural as your heart beating or your lungs filling. I know a few spells, picked up over the centuries, but generally leave such things to wizards. Only evil men use the black arts and I'm not an evil man."

Mina shivered. His rumbling tone did something wicked to her senses. He didn't touch her, but she wanted him to. Her breathing deepened and her body tingled like when he pressed himself to her. She glanced at his mouth, wanting him to kiss her again. All other thoughts fled.

"And I stare at you, Lady Willamina," he said, drawing closer still so that his warm breath hit upon her ear. "I stare because you are very beautiful to behold and I would look at you. I stare because when you allowed me to kiss you it was pure ecstasy and I wish to do it again. I stare because I can think of little else than claiming your body with mine right here, right now."

Larus drew back, studying Mina carefully, obviously unashamed by his bold admission. She stared straight ahead, boring her gaze into his muscled, bare shoulder. Her mouth opened and then shut, opened again, closed once more. Blinking rapidly, she dared a glance at his face. The devilish curl to his lip lifted one corner and his eyes were bright with passion.

"You... you shouldn't say such things," Mina answered weakly. "It isn't proper."

"Humans," he chuckled darkly and Mina wondered at the disapproval in his tone. "You haven't changed much. You still can't be honest about what you feel, what you want. I smell your desire for me, so there is no point in denying it, and yet you do."

"What separates us humans from the animals, my lord, is that we don't act on pure instinct and impulses. Part of being evolved is that we have the capacity to be civilized and mannered," she answered.

"Much good that's done you." Larus laughed. "The lot of you are scared and repressed. Like angry children you strike first, think later, and pretend it's all in the name of what's holy. That's one of the reasons we sealed off your realm from ours because you kept wishing to fight us without cause. Tell me. Are your kingdoms still at war? Have you finally achieved peace?"

Mina thought of her home and paled. Everything she loved was taken away by politics and wars. Yes, they were at war—always at war. For lack of a better defense, she crossed her arms over her chest and tapped her foot, stating, "We are not childish. We fight because we must. And I think it's very likely we ran your kind from our realm with your tail between your legs like cowards."

"Do you know how humans came to be?" Larus asked. "You were a spell gone awry with a group of wizards. They tried to create a new food source for the dragons—only the dragons didn't like the taste of you.

The Haeven order is still shunned to this day because of it. That is what your kind evolved from."

"Blasphemy." Mina spat.

"To whose gods? Yours or mine?" Larus chuckled though he didn't seem to be in a humorous mood. "I assure you, my lady, I've spoken to mine and they're quite amused by it."

"Are your kingdoms any better? I'd bet you my life that your kings are just as greedy as ours, just as deceitful. Do you think your king cares about what happens to you?" Mina stopped, wondering at his strange look. When he didn't answer, she said, "I thought not. Listen, I don't wish to debate you on which of our kind is better. It's obvious you don't wish for us to be here and I don't wish to stay. Let us focus on that, my lord. Now, if we've come to this realm, there must be a way to get back."

"The portals." Larus straightened.

"Good," Mina answered, thinking that they were making progress. "Will you please take us there?"

"No." Larus turned from her to walk down the path.

"No?" Mina gasped, following him. "What do you mean, no?"

"No, I won't take you to the portals, at least not yet. We must first figure out why and how you came to be here."

"What does it matter?"

"It matters because if a portal is opened, then more of you can come through it." Larus let her fall into step next to him. "If I show them to you, perhaps you will tell others about them."

"Why would I want to?" Mina asked. "They would think me touched."

Larus chuckled. "Long ago, your kind tried to use the immortals for their selfish gain. Magic is strong but must always be in balance. Humans sought to harness it without considering the repercussions. They could have destroyed us all."

"Then where do you take us?"

"To see the elders so that they," Larus glanced down at her with shaded eyes, "and the lycan king may decide what to do with you."

Mina stopped. Fear clamped over her heart. She'd lived through what one king's will had done to her and her family, and she wouldn't stand by to let it happen again. Sophia was all she had left. "And what will this king do if it's decided we can't go back? What will happen to us then?"

Larus studied her carefully. She was so beautiful, but he could feel the hurt and anger in her. It was strange that he would feel so many of her emotions as if they were his own. He'd felt drawn to her from the beginning. The connection grew stronger with each passing hour, and every fiber in his being wanted to offer her protection.

"Your kind can't survive in our world without protection," Larus said softly. "It would be cruel to set you free in it."

"Then we are to be killed." Her tone was flat. "That is what kings do to inconvenient people."

Larus frowned that she would automatically conclude they meant her harm. What had happened to her and Sophia to make her so hard? It was clear she thought little of rulers, but that was hardly his doing. He'd meant that she would more than likely be expected to find a mate amongst his people, or one of the other compatible races.

"Why not, right? What's the life of two humans—creatures that you so obviously despise?" Mina shook her head. "Men, you're all the same. It matters not the race. Tell me, is there a realm of just women? I'd gladly go there. Have you a portal? For I am sure it is a better place than here or my world."

Mina began walking faster, trying to move past him up the path. He glanced around. Sophia was ahead in a nearby field picking flowers and singing to herself. Before he could stop to think, he grabbed Mina's arm and jerked her back. She gasped in surprise and he took the opening, crushing his mouth down hard onto her parted lips. She struggled lightly. But as he moved his tongue to dip past her teeth, her resistance faded. A soft moan left her lips, washing pleasantly into his mouth, stirring his blood with pure instinctive lust.

She moved her hands up to his shoulders, resting lightly against his bare flesh. Larus pulled her closer, liking the way her softer body fit next to him as if the gods had carved her for him. His body lurched, his member hard with need. The primal urge to take her grew strong, and he pulled her tighter against him, rocking his hips into her belly. He met with the soft globe of her breast, kneading it in firm strokes until her nipple budded to press into his palm.

Mina gasped and struggled. His kisses trailed from her lush lips to her tender neck. Her resistance to her passion only awoke the beast within him. Larus was a man known for his ease and control, but somehow this woman took his control and tossed it aside. The beast wanted to hunt, to play her game as she refused to give in to what they both wanted. He smelled her longing, a pleasing fragrance in his head, tempting and teasing him. The beast wanted her blood as well as her sweet body. He wanted to ravish her, mark her, bite her, claim her. The last surprised him and he forced himself to let her go. He gasped for breath, but it was hard to control his raging desire.

Mina stood before him, wide-eyed and scared. She trembled, but didn't scream, didn't run. "Why... why did you do that?"

Larus frowned. How could he possibly understand her question? All he could think about was how he wanted to toss her to the ground and ride her hard until they both met their release. A groan left him at the thought and he mindlessly reached for her again.

13

MINA JERKED AWKWARDLY, TERRIFIED BY THE creature before her. At first, his kiss had been sweet, passionate, and even enjoyable. But then, he changed, turning almost rough. Mina shivered. It had still been incredibly pleasant, but the very intensity of the feelings scared her.

When she looked at him, his eyes were gold-green, his teeth slightly elongated as if he would become the beast. With trembling fingers she touched her neck. It burned where he kissed her. She withdrew her hand to find it covered with blood.

"What have you done?" she asked, looking at her hand and then into his eyes. He blinked, only looking at her hand when she held it up for inspection. Her fingers shaking, she repeated louder, "What have you done?"

"Mina?" Sophia asked, sounding concerned. "Mina?"

"What have you done?" Mina insisted, not hearing her sister.

Larus opened his mouth as if he would speak. Mina shook. Sophia was suddenly by Larus's side, looking at her. He quickly wiped his lips before Sophia saw the blood on them.

"Mina, you cut yourself," Sophia scolded. The woman shook her head, sighed, and leaned over to rip a section of her skirt. Crossing to Mina, Sophia began humming as she wrapped the cloth around Mina's throat. "You should be more careful, Mina. It's a good thing my knight was here to save you, or else you might have really been hurt."

Mina nodded. Sophia seemed unaware of the fact that Larus was still partly shifted into a wolf. When Sophia finished her bandage, she pulled back and nodded.

"There," Sophia said. "All taken care of. Oh, my flowers!"

Sophia took off jogging back down the path. Mina followed her, making an arc past Larus. She didn't want to be alone with him again.

"Mina," he said. When she glanced at him, his face

was back to normal, his eyes sorrowful. "Mina, I'm sorry."

Mina shook and nodded her head at the same time, unsure if she accepted the apology or not. Hurrying past, she found Sophia picking her discarded flowers up from the ground. Her sister glanced at her, smiling brightly.

"Do you think my love will like these?" Sophia asked, holding up the purple and yellow plants.

"Sophia," Mina said, shivering. She pushed her hair over her shoulder. "You need to stay away from him. Please."

Sophia's face fell and Mina could see her sister would argue.

"Men like to pursue women they think they can't have, remember? Pretend you don't want him and he will want you," Mina rushed, trying to manipulate her sister into compliance. "Stay away from him."

Sophia considered that. "You are very wise, Mina. I shall try it. Men do like to chase, do they not?"

Mina nodded, hoping that her advice would keep Sophia away from Larus and safe from the spell until she figured out a way to break free. "Oh, yes. That's why they're men."

"Well, I shall certainly do that," Sophia said, nodding her head. Mina sighed with relief, only to stop as her sister added, "Just as soon as I give my love these flowers he wanted."

"Sophia, wait—" Mina frowned, watching the long trail of blonde hair as her sister ran down the path to Larus. She didn't want to follow, didn't want to face him, but she had no choice. She couldn't leave Sophia alone with him.

When she returned, Larus was still standing pretty much in the same spot, looking at her sister in annoyance as he took the flowers. As she neared, his eyes instantly went to her face, gauging her reaction to him. Mina looked away.

"Shouldn't we get going?" Mina asked, staring down the path. "I'd like to see if these elders can get us home."

"I don't want to go home." Sophia pouted, nearing tears. "Mina, no. I want to stay here with my Larus."

Mina closed her eyes and sighed, not saying a word.

They walked in silence until Mina was sure her legs were going to fall out from underneath her. Sophia didn't seem to notice, doing her best to provoke Larus's jealousy. It was almost sickening to watch her enthralled sister make a mild spectacle of herself. However as long as Sophia kept chattering endless nonsense about her old suitors—suitors who in reality probably could no longer remember her name since their father's death—Mina was saved from being drawn into conversation.

"Yes, I have many suitors," Sophia sighed for the fifth or sixth time, batting her eyelashes at Larus.

Finally, when it became obvious she wasn't going to let up, he sighed loudly and said in exasperation, "Yes, I understand. I gladly bow out. I wish you much happiness with one of them."

Sophia paled, looking at Mina in panic. She stopped and shook her head. "No, no, you are the most treasured of those suitors, Larus. Do not give up, my love. If you ask me, I will be your bride."

It was Larus's turn to pale. Sophia stopped, smiling expectantly as if she waited for him to swoop down to one knee and declare his affection. Mina snorted as she tried to hold back her laughter. When she glanced back, Larus was glaring at her.

Taking pity on him, Mina asked, "Will there be a stream nearby our next encampment? I should like to bathe."

Larus's glare turned into a grateful look of relief. "Yes, of course. I'll show you."

Mina watched as he quickly continued down the path, brushing past her to walk ahead of them. Sophia came by her side and grabbed her arm. "Mina, do you think something is wrong with him? Why didn't he ask me to be his bride?"

He's sane, Mina thought dryly.

Sophia sighed, pulling on Mina's arm to follow him. "I was so sure he was going to ask me. It's very curious. Perhaps, I should try harder."

14

LARUS FROWNED AS HE STORMED THROUGH THE forest to look for firewood. The moon was half full, shining the most exquisite silver over the land through the tops of the trees. The giant orb would shift its colors with the magic of the seasons, but the season of the silver moon lasted the longest. The air was beginning to warm, the odd chill he'd felt the other day was gone.

Leaving the infuriating women at the campsite to rest, he knew he needed a break from them. It was late in the evening and he felt as far away from the elders as when he started that morning. Human pace was excruciatingly slow, but he had no choice in the matter. He had no wish to carry them both on his back. Mina's soft thighs around him would be too much, and one could only guess at how Sophia would act.

Larus wasn't sure taking them before the council was the best course of action, but what else could he do with them? He'd only said the elders because he had to tell Mina something. How could he expect her to follow him, if he admitted he didn't know what he was going to do? If he knew, he would have used the mind link to try to call Ilar or Malak to him for help. For some reason, he didn't. He was pretty sure that reason was a very beautiful dark-haired temptress named Willamina. He didn't want to share her yet, especially not with the charming womanizer Malak, even if that meant putting up with Sophia in the meantime.

He would have to decide tomorrow. The paths would fork and he could take them straight to Lycaon, north to the elders, or south to Malak at Fenris and a known portal. Such complete confusion was a new feeling for the lycan king and he didn't like it. It didn't help that Mina's scent was in his head, and her taste was in his mouth—both her passionate kiss and her blood.

His stomach knotted every time he saw Mina's bandaged throat. What had gotten into him that he didn't even remember biting her? That the beast had come out without his knowledge or control was madness. Only after he calmed his raging desires, did he register the potently sweet flavor of her blood on his lips.

The most damning thing was that she was now

marked as his lover—or at least marked to be his lover since they had yet to come together. Her pull would become stronger and harder to resist. He was afraid if he didn't slake his desire for her soon the beast would surface and take her by any means necessary. The king didn't like being helpless.

If they crossed paths with anyone familiar with his kind, they'd sense her status and news would spread that Larus had taken a mortal woman as his—even if it was temporary. However, temporary lovers were rarely marked without reason, for once marked it was harder to break the bond. Both parties had to wish the separation, and Larus knew his body wouldn't be listening to his head for some time yet.

Looking down at the stiff mass between his legs, he sighed. It had been like that since their first kiss. He was thankful his tunic draped forward to cover it from view, not that Mina looked at him more than a handful of times since the incident. Larus winced. He would hate for Sophia to think it was for her.

His hands shook and he couldn't concentrate. Looking around the forest, Larus wondered if he should take care of matters on his own. It couldn't hurt to try. Dropping the firewood, he leaned his shoulder against a tree and sniffed the air. No one was around to bear witness.

Slowly, he lifted his tunic and fisted his hand over his shaft, stroking in firm pulls. His eyes drifted closed as Mina's smell came to him. She heard her sultry voice in his head, though it wasn't hard and defiant like when she'd talked to him, it was soft and yielding like when she'd kissed him. He moved faster, stroking over the entire length, building his body toward a much needed release. A soft moan caught in his throat. He saw her face, felt her lush lips against him. Imagining her mouth was on his erection, his body jerked. He instantly spilled his seed onto the forest floor.

Gasping for breath, feeling relieved now that the pressure was lessened, he let his tunic fall once more over his body. He turned, leaning to rest his back against the rough bark of the tree. His actions helped to ease some of his body's tension but did nothing to temper his desire for Mina.

Hearing a light whispering noise and detecting the scent of old death on the evening breeze, Larus stiffened. He narrowed his eyes, taking in the surrounding forest. A chill ran over him, urging him to shift. He resisted, staying where he was.

"I thought I detected someone out," a low, smooth voice said. The words sounded bored.

Larus turned, looking at the old vampire who addressed him. The creature had shoulder length black hair that hung around his striking face. The dark locks streaked across his overly pale flesh, stirring in the breeze. His gray eyes were rimmed with red, attesting to a recent feed. Larus's stomach tensed, as he thought of Mina and her sister. They'd make a tempting meal for a vampire. He'd been so preoccupied with lust that he hadn't been concentrating on them.

"Devlin," Larus acknowledged with a stiff nod, not giving away his thoughts.

"So, what honor do I owe that the great lycan king pays me a visit?" Devlin asked, smiling without real pleasure. When he moved, it was with deceptive ease. Larus knew that this man could strike fast if he so chose. He wasn't scared for himself, so much as the human women under his protection.

"I'm merely passing through the forest," Larus answered, keeping his tone level. "I'll be off your land tomorrow."

"Why not run past as your kind normally does?" Devlin questioned. "I wonder why you stop."

"No reason," Larus lied.

Devlin's smile deepened, though his eyes still looked bored. "So, the human women are not yours? They are unclaimed?"

Larus tensed. Devlin knew about the sisters. He

wondered what the vampire would do, what he might have done already. "They are mine."

"Both?" Devlin questioned.

"Yes, both," Larus allowed.

"Only one bears your mark," Devlin countered. "The blonde child seems to be unclaimed."

"Believe me, Devlin, she is trouble you don't want." Larus made a move to leave.

Devlin lifted a hand to stop him. The vampire sniffed and looked to the ground where Larus had spilled his seed. His grin deepened and his gray eyes lit with interest. Larus much preferred the vampire's boredom.

"You have a marked woman nearby, a beautiful one at that, and yet you spill your manhood on the ground?" Devlin asked, his dark brow lifting in question.

Larus didn't speak. He didn't have to.

"It has been a long while since I've tasted human blood," Devlin said. "I wonder, has it changed its flavor? You must know for you've tasted the dark one."

"It's the same." Larus shrugged. He made a move to walk toward the camp. "Weak, as all mortals are."

"Hmm," Devlin sighed, turning as if to walk with Larus. "Let me have the blonde one, for a taste. Consider it an exchange for safe passage over my land."

"The wars are over," Larus said. "I can pass so long as I don't linger."

"A lycan staying the night could be considered lingering. You could always run ahead, but that would leave the two mortals unprotected and I could then claim the blonde one just the same." Devlin lifted his long nails and studied them. They looked perfectly manicured and thin, but Larus knew they'd be as durable as his claws. "Come on, one taste of her. What do you care? You don't take her as yours."

"No, I'm sorry." Larus looked at Devlin in warning.

"Ah, then, so am I." Devlin chuckled. He stepped back and bowed like a true gentleman. Before he'd even pulled back up, his body dissolved into a fine mist, spreading out over the forest. A second later Sophia's yell sounded. Larus tensed, running toward the campsite. When he got there, Mina stared at Devlin.

The vampire had his hand on Sophia's arm as she struggled against him. Mina charged, but Devlin lifted his hand and pushed her back without touching her. She stumbled into Larus's chest. He caught her, holding her back as she again sought to free her sister. He smelled her fear and felt her anger as she bravely tried to fight the old vampire.

"Devlin," Larus said, his eyes darkening.

Sophia yelled again and repeatedly hit the vampire's arms. Devlin didn't even flinch. In fact, he looked amused. Swinging Sophia around to face him, he let his eyes swirl with color. Sophia instantly quieted and stared up at him, becoming compliant. Her arms rose about his neck and she offered her lips up.

Devlin grinned but didn't kiss her. He glanced at Larus, and said, "I love a woman with fire."

"Sophia?" Mina panicked, still tugging to free herself. "Larus, what's going on? Help her. Let me go."

"You shouldn't have been so greedy, friend, all I wanted was a taste of her, now I will take more. I'll take this prize with me, so that you may play with the other. Enjoy your night and then come to my home tomorrow evening at dusk, no sooner, to pick up this enchanting creature. I am sure I will grow tired of her by then." Devlin petted Sophia's silky blonde hair, lifting the locks to his mouth for a gentle kiss. His eyes bore into Sophia's and she moaned weakly in response, resting her head on his shoulder. Devlin scooped her up, hooking his arm under her to carry her before him.

"Let her go, you devil." Mina screamed. "Release her."

Before Larus could protest, Devlin's body whispered over the wind, moving so fast it looked as if he blurred into nothingness, taking Sophia with him.

Larus's grip tightened on Mina's arms, as he held her back. He knew if he made a scene and fought Devlin's right to pursue the unclaimed woman, he'd risk harming both sisters in the fray. If he let Sophia go with him and did nothing, Devlin would take her, drink from her—hopefully making it pleasurable—and then try to seduce her. If she didn't succumb, she'd be free to go.

"Sophia." Mina yelled. Larus let go of her and she ran to where the vampire had been.

"No, Mina, do not," Larus ordered, darting forward to grab her arm when she would run into the forest. "He won't hurt her. He wants..."

"What?" she asked. "What does he want with Sophia? Is he the one who brought us here? What is he?"

"That is a vampire," Larus said. "And he wants a taste of your sister, that is all. If we let him have it, he won't harm her."

"A taste?" Mina gasped in disbelief, her hand flying to her throat to where her wound was covered with the bandage. She shook her head, backing away. "Blood?"

Larus stiffened, reminded of how connected they were. "Yes, blood."

Mina's hand didn't leave her neck. She continued to stare. "You said if we stayed with you, you would protect us. You call this protection?"

"Mina." Larus took a step toward her. He lifted his hand in offering. "He won't harm her. I've known Devlin many years, and he isn't a cruel being, not for a vampire."

"Not for a vampire," Mina repeated, reading too well

the meaning of that phrase. She looked into his eyes. "I have your word that Sophia will be fine?"

"Yes." Larus nodded. Devlin wouldn't kill Sophia, not after only a night. The old vampire had been instrumental in calling a truce to the vampire and lycan war, even though he held no love for the lycan kind. Larus didn't want to tell Mina he suspected it was his fault Sophia was taken. In a twisted sense, Devlin probably thought he was doing the lycan king a favor—albeit with a selfish benefit—taking Sophia so that Larus could be alone to pursue Mina without interruption.

Mina's bottom lip trembled and, to his surprise, she rushed forward. She passed his offered hand and threw her arms about his neck, hugging him. His body responded to hers instantly, becoming aroused. He slowly drew his arms in to hold her. The sweet smell of her filled him, tainted by dust.

"I'll hold you to your word," she said, pressing her face into his chest. "If you lie, I'll kill you."

"Sophia will be treated well. She'll be fed, given a bath and clothing." Larus stroked down Mina's dark hair. "Actually, she'll probably rest better than out here with us. I would not be surprised if she remembers nothing of her time there. Come, it grows dark. There's a stream nearby where you can bathe."

Mina pulled back and nodded, seeming resigned to

what she couldn't change. Larus reached over and grabbed his cloak from the ground. He was reluctant to let her go, but if he kept holding her, he'd start kissing her and this time he doubted he'd stop at just that. Feeling a shiver over his skin and the dilatation of his eyes as they flickered dangerously with gold, he fought down the beast that would surface.

"This way," he said gruffly, turning to the forest to go to the stream.

15

Mina watched Larus walk away. Whatever possessed her to trust his word? Eyeing his strong back, she followed him. Even though she was scared for her sister, she felt confident that Sophia would be all right. She'd looked into Larus's green eyes and had felt a calmness coming over her. She felt safe.

Mina stayed close as he led her to a stream. There was enough silver moonlight to see by, so she had no problem keeping up. The sound of gently flowing water surrounded them. Larus laid the cloak on the shore and turned to study her. Mina wondered if he was going to stay and strangely hoping he would.

"I'll keep my back to you," he said, confirming he had no intention of leaving her alone in the dark forest. "Call out if you have a need of me."

Mina nodded, and he turned away from her. She slowly stripped from her dress. She kept her eyes focused on his back, remembering the feel of his body when he held her. A tingling erupted in her limbs, making her want to be near him. The cool night air brushed her skin, and she shivered. Keeping one eye on him to make sure he didn't peek, and slightly disappointed when he didn't, Mina touched her toe into the water. She was surprised to find it warm.

"There's nothing in here, right?" she asked.

"I don't sense anything," he answered, sniffing the air. "Merfolk sometimes pass on their way to the ocean, but it's unlikely they'd be here this time of year."

"Merfolk?" Mina asked, walking deeper into the water.

"Half fish, half man or woman," Larus answered. "I assure you they are harmless."

"Ah." Mina lowered her body, feeling oddly exhilarated by the idea of him so close and herself so naked. The warm water encased her skin, only adding to the heat his nearness put inside her stomach. She kept talking, wanting to hear his voice. "Are they very big?"

"Average." Larus shrugged.

"I wish I had soap," Mina sighed wistfully. She rubbed her hands over her body, doing her best to scrub clean. Her eyes were glued on his back, roaming freely over his exposed calves and his firm butt beneath the tunic. She shivered, wishing he'd turn around and disrobe so she may look him over thoroughly. The image of him crouched before her without a stitch of clothing was burned into her mind. She'd been too stunned to memorize every detail like she wanted.

"I'll get you something. Don't worry. I won't be far." Mina wondered at the hoarseness of his voice as he said the words. Watching as he disappeared into the forest, she grew nervous, but he came back a few seconds later. He walked with his head down, watching his feet. "I won't look."

He lifted his hand when he reached the side of the stream and he held out what looked to be the inside of an overlarge daisy. She stepped forward to meet him. When she stood a few feet away, she stopped, not moving to take it.

"What does it do?" she asked. Was her voice hoarse as well now?

"Break it open. The liquid inside can be used to cleanse." His words were low and strained.

"Do you not want to look at me?" she asked softly, flushing with embarrassment.

Larus's eyes darted up at the question. Mina tried to

smile, but it was hard under his penetrating gaze. She didn't move, and he seemed to take her stillness as permission. Slowly, almost hesitantly, his eyes moved down over her throat. Beads of water clung to her flesh, awash with moonlight and glistening like stars. His breathing deepened.

Mina took a bold step forward and grabbed the soap. Then, backing into the stream once more, she cracked it open. A sweet fragrance assaulted her from the flower bud. Holding the broken halves in one hand, she dipped her fingers inside to get them wet and began rubbing her arms. The soap tingled where it touched her and she smiled.

Larus turned from her, his motions stiff. Mina scrubbed her body, feeling the tingling of soap everywhere. Her flesh pulsed with life. Larus's back was again to her, and he didn't speak. Rubbing the flower into her hair, she lowered into the stream to rinse when she suddenly stopped. Looking around, she shook nervously.

"*Ahh,*" she screamed, trying to sound alarmed. She made a run for Larus. He spun around, and she flung herself into his warm chest. "Something... something in the water. I felt... by my foot."

Larus looked at the stream and then to her. To her pleasure, his hands slid over her hips to hold her next to him. He glanced up at her soapy hair. "I detect nothing."

One naked, soapy breast slid halfway off his tunic and pressed tightly to his chest. When she breathed, she felt the texture of his hot skin caressing her, making the tip ache unbearably. Instinctively, she wanted to feel more.

"I felt something," Mina insisted, clinging tighter and liking the way it brought her body up hard to his. She felt his arousal pressing into her softer stomach but didn't pull away. She shook to be so near him. "I'm scared. Would you come in and make sure it's nothing so I can rinse my hair?"

Larus looked deep into her eyes. Slowly, he nodded. Mina forced herself to let him go, unable to tear her gaze away from him as he kicked off his boots. As he unknotted the tunic at his shoulder and the material fell to the ground, she gasped. His large shaft was fully erect.

His gaze flickered with gold determination, making her heart beat violently against the walls of her chest. He took a stalking step forward and Mina instantly kept away from him, going into the water once more. When she reached the middle, she stopped. He came before her, looking down over her body without touching.

Mina slowly lowered herself into the stream, watching his muscled chest and defined stomach pass by her vision as she knelt to rinse her hair. He edged forward even more, bringing his arousal closer to her face. She hesitated, before leaning her head back and going beneath the surface.

Mina rinsed, staying close to him. Breaking the surface, she rubbed the water from her eyes. She wondered why he made no move to touch her. His skin was dark, marred by a few scars, but nothing that detracted from his handsomeness. Not knowing what came over her, she leaned forward and brushed a kiss onto the side of his hip. He didn't move.

Mina grew bolder when he didn't pull away. She glided her hands over his legs, coming up from beneath the water. Caressing the outsides of his thighs, she moved her hands over his solid hips to his waist. She kept her eyes on him, liking the fire that burned within his green gaze.

She kissed him again, this time on the front of his hip. His stomach contracted and his arousal lurched at the motion. Curious, she brushed her lips to him once more, closer to his navel. His hips jerked forward, causing her hands to slip around to the backs of his thighs. Unable to resist, she let her fingers explore the hard cheeks she found there.

"Mina," he said, low and possessive.

"Do you want me to stop?" She instantly pulled her hands off him. Her lips pressed nervously together. Had she done something wrong? Was she not supposed to kiss him like that? Touch him? Did he not want her to? She was no fool. She knew what would happen, what she asked for—for the most part. When he didn't answer, only continued to breathe heavily, she asked, "Do you find me hideous because I am human? Is that it?"

A tear slipped over her cheek. A few days ago, she'd never known a creature like him could exist. Now, she couldn't think of ever living without him. It was strange, but when he bit her, she felt as if he connected himself to her.

"I apologize, my lord, I-I'm not myself. I must be under a spell like Sophia." Her words were weak, shaking so badly they could barely be understood. Mina moved to stand, wanting to get away from his rejection, wanting to hide her shame.

Larus's hand shot out to stop her. He tightly gripped her upper arm. His words a low growl, he said, "You are not under a spell. I won't have you believing that is why you desire me."

Mina opened her mouth to protest, but Larus's kiss crushed down on her, grinding passionately against her lips until she trembled and fell against him. She moaned lightly, rubbing her naked body into his chest. He was so hot.

His hips flexed forward, rocking into her. A growl sounded in the back of his throat. Larus's hands were everywhere at once, running up and down her frame, cupping her backside, drawing her body closer.

"Argh," he groaned, pulling his mouth away.

His eyes hot, he kept her tight to his body as he tried to regain control. Her flesh was so frail, so malleable against his harder length. She was slender, smooth, and so soft. He took a deep breath and then another, trying to force the picture of her from his mind—her ripe breasts budded with pink nipples, her parted thighs, the thatch of dark hair between them begging to be touched, kissed, licked. She'd taken the strip of cloth from her neck and it appeared she'd healed almost completely from the wound. The sight of her was nearly as torturous as the smell coming from her thighs.

Larus didn't remember humans being so supple. It had been a long time since he had felt such softness or such longing. She was so cold and fragile compared to the hot-blooded lycan. Gruffly, he said, "Come."

Grabbing Mina's hand, he took quick steps as he led her to shore. Instinctively, he knew she was innocent to the ways of men. The knowledge only made her reaction to his touch all the more pure. He took his cloak and laid it out over the ground. Then, pulling her forward, he kissed her anew before urging her onto her knees.

"Continue," he said harshly, almost as an order. He took a deep breath, forcing his arms to stay back.

Mina looked up at him. They were in the same position as they'd been in the water. She touched him, gliding her hands boldly as she discovered the feel of him. Her mouth brushed soft kisses along his hip and waist, liking the power she felt when he groaned and jerked for more. His fists clenched tightly at his sides.

When she continued her light teasing, getting close to his arousal only to keep away, he reached forward, guiding her to him. She kissed his hard shaft, surprised by how much hotter it was than the rest of him.

"*Ahh*," he cried out, hoarse and panting. His hand on her hair tightened. "I have to stop you or you'll finish me."

Before Mina could understand his words, she was pressed on her back with his weight on top of her. He began kissing her, moving down over her neck. She stiffened as he neared the bite mark. Slowly, he licked it.

"I'm sorry for this," he said.

"I want you to do it again," Mina said in return, astonished that the words even escaped her lips.

He growled but didn't bite. "Don't offer that to me for I'm already tempted."

Larus moved his hands over her breasts, soon joining them with his journeying mouth. He sucked and pinched her nipples in turn, sometimes doing both at once as he used his mouth and hands together. Glorious sensations flooded her, running a rampant course through her blood.

Only when her hands worked erratically over his back and arms did he move lower, licking a hot trail to her navel. He rimmed the small hole with his tongue before drawing his wet kisses lower. He glided his hand along her hips, pulling toward her inner thighs. Mina tensed, instinctively drawing her thighs together to hide herself from view. Larus groaned and pushed her legs apart.

Before she could react, he latched his mouth onto her, rolling his tongue along the sensitive clit he found hidden within her folds. Mina had never felt anything like it. As if by a will of their own, her hips were pushing up to his mouth for more. His long tongue worked lower, and she swore she felt it dip intimately inside her, reaching up as he stoked the flames he ignited. She rocked harder, riding his thrusting tongue as he held her hips and showed her how to set the pace.

"Oh," she cried out for more. "*Larus.*"

He groaned louder, and she passionately called out his name. His fingers moved, replacing his tongue in her wet, silken depths. They were firmer and felt even better riding up to touch her.

Larus growled, letting her know that he loved the feel of her. Her body was tight around his finger, but it felt so good she couldn't think to stop. When she cried out, riding his hand willingly, he slipped in a second finger, stretching her more. She called out his name, over and over. As if unable to stop, he slipped in a third finger.

Mina tensed. She felt full but wanted more. His mouth continued its intimate massage as she rode his hand. His fingers curled within her. It was almost as if she could feel his desire for her inside her body, magnifying her pleasure. She reached out, wanting to find the end of her torment. Her body shook as if everything she felt built into one extraordinary moment of perfection.

"Larus," she pleaded weakly, her whole body jerking as he brought forth her pleasure. At the sound, he pulled out. She clutched for him. "No, don't go. Please, don't stop doing that."

He had no intention of leaving, as he brought his body over hers. The tip of his shaft dipped along her moist center, parting her still trembling lips as he aligned his body. His hand on her breast and his lips on her neck, he pushed forward, slowly gliding into her tight passage, stretching her open even more.

"Oh," Mina gasped, panting wildly as she tried to think straight. She couldn't. The pressure built until she thought she'd rip in two if he went any deeper. Then, with a strong push, he sank himself in, burying his shaft to the hilt.

"Temptress Mina," he groaned, a conquering sound of complete satisfaction. "You feel so good, so soft."

The initial pain subsided quickly as he moved, thrusting himself in and out of her body. There was something to his smell, his presence that took away every doubt, every sense of pain or fear. The tension built anew, intense and mind-numbing. She was soon writhing against him for more, meeting his thrusts.

Larus pumped his hips. She felt that he was holding back and whimpered in protest. There was a connection between them, as if she felt his thoughts, knew him, understood him. She met him thrust for thrust. The beast inside him took over, swirling in his eyes and elongating his teeth. The pace of his thrusts became almost frantic and hard. The thick arousal inside her seemed to expand and lengthen with the subtle change. His lips parted, and he bit her neck. She moaned and didn't fight it as he took her blood. He tensed and she knew it was all he could do not to ram her soft body into the ground.

His passion for her was too much. Her tight passage quivered around him. The second her body started to climax he let loose. His hips jerked as his seed filled her.

Mina gasped softly, clutching him as she continued to spasm and clench. Larus pushed and pulled, milking the orgasm from her body, even as his was spent. Her body's cream and her sweet blood were mixed together on his lips when he kissed her.

"I think you're wrong," she said, panting as she tried to regain her breath. His weight pressed into her, covering but not heavy. "I have to be under a spell. I feel numb all over, except for my heart which is pounding violently."

"It's no spell," he denied, lifting to look at her. She smiled at him, raising her hands to him in acceptance. Larus relaxed. "We should get you back to the fire."

Mina sat up as he pulled off her completely. She thought of Sophia and instantly felt guilty for what she'd done. Here she was experiencing one of the most heavenly acts she never dreamed possible, and her sister was locked away with some vampire.

Larus turned and glanced at her and she hid her expression from him, not wanting him to see her vulnerability or her guilt. Pulling the cloak around her naked body as she stood, she walked over to grab her dress and shoes. She had no desire to put the dirty clothes back on.

"I'm going to wash these and hang them to dry." Mina went to the stream and rinsed them the best she could. She also cleaned her neck, surprised to find there were no wounds this time. Her body was sore, but not in an entirely unpleasant way.

When she finished, she found Larus had draped his

tunic over himself once more and held his boots in his hands. He searched her face, and she coolly met his eyes.

Mina guiltily thought of her sister, even as she wished for him to say something tender to her. He turned, leading the way back to the fire. Neither one of them said a word.

16

Sophia blinked, looking around the elegant castle chamber. Red and black silk draped the walls, even where there was nothing to hide but stone. She had instructions from Lord Devlin's manservant, a little green creature, that she was to await his master. Her host had left her to bathe and had even given her a fresh change of clothes.

The gown was beautiful—a rich burgundy with gold embroidery along the edges. A queen would surely wear such clothes. The square neckline was low, showing off the tops of her rounded breasts. The waist was made to fit tight, but as she was so skinny from their scarce diet the last year, it hung a little loose on her frame. The full skirt moved when she walked, splitting up the front to reveal a cream linen underskirt.

Tilting her head to the side, she hummed lightly. Her head swam, but it wasn't with thoughts, so much as the knowledge she loved Larus and wanted to see him. But, at the same time, she thought to love Devlin. His beautiful eyes swirled with such silver promise. It was strange that she could go from wanting no men in her life, to loving two of them with what had to be her whole heart. But Sophia didn't have the will to question it.

Sighing, she turned as Lord Devlin came into the chamber without knocking. He smiled at her, looking her over. He was graceful, elegant. His dark clothing looked strange, the black silk tunic buttoned down the front. Unlike Larus, he wore pants. They too were black but didn't look to be silk. The color complemented his skin. Lifting his hand, he gestured her to stand. She did, walking toward him without hesitation.

"You're not frightened?" he asked.

"No," she said simply. "I love you. But, I'm torn, for I also love my Larus."

Devlin frowned. When she stood in front of him, her glassy insipid gaze looking up at his face without fear or emotion, he leaned down. He purposefully stopped mesmerizing her. "Are you sure you love us both?"

"Actually, as I think on it, I think I love Larus more. Would you take me to him?" Sophia asked. "I miss him."

"You're enchanted," Devlin said flatly, pulling away.

"Thank you," Sophia said, not really listening. "Doesn't my Larus have the most enchanting smile?"

"I've never looked at the lycan king in such a way, my dear." Devlin chuckled dryly.

"No, not the lycan king," Sophia said. "My Larus. I don't know the king. Don't you think Larus brave and true?"

Devlin smiled. "Who put you under this spell? Do you remember?"

"My Larus," Sophia sighed. "I'm under his spell. One look and my heart was lost to him."

"One look," he mused. Devlin allowed his eyes to swirl again and her mouth fell open as she stared lovingly at him.

"You are brave and handsome as well, my love," Sophia said, batting her eyelashes. "Don't be jealous. I love you, too."

"Show me your neck," he said, not even bothering to hide his amusement at her words. "I wish to have a taste of you."

Sophia instantly obeyed tilting her head to the side, smiling brightly. Devlin touched her face, holding her still as he leaned down to drink. She didn't even flinch.

17

"Do you have a family who will be looking for you?" Larus asked, tossing a twig into the fire and watching it burn. He kept his expression guarded. The act of coming inside her, coupled with his bite, claimed her even more as his lover. He knew no one from his world would dare touch her so long as she carried the lycan king's unmistakable scent.

Resting on her side, Mina stared into the dancing flames. Her dress lay drying across a low branch near the fire so she was naked beneath his thick cloak. She blinked in surprise at his words. They hadn't spoken since their joining by the stream. Sitting up, she hugged the soft material around her shoulders. He could feel the turmoil in her, as he felt her renewing desire for him. She fought it still, but their passion was growing bigger than the both of them.

"Why do you ask?" she inquired after a pause.

Larus's gaze bore into her, studying her carefully. He sat a few feet away. She seemed nervous, and he was sorry for it. It was possible she didn't know what to say to him after what had happened. She'd been untouched before him and he'd given no indication of his feelings on the matter. But he would not embarrass her by speaking on it until she said something first. "I'm curious. Do you have anyone who would be looking for you?"

He could sense that Mina thought about lying, but was relieved when she instead spoke the truth, "No. Sophia is all I have."

"No father? Mother? Brothers?"

Mina's face turned hard. She pulled the cloak tighter. "No. My mother died having my sister. We are the only two. We have no brothers."

"And your father?"

"Why do you care?" Her tone was a bit too harsh.

"Why do you not answer?" he insisted, keeping his words level.

"He died two years ago," Mina said. "Sophia and I have been alone ever since."

"That's why you fought the wild animal for meat? Because you were starved?" Larus probed. Mina nodded.

He didn't need her confirmation. He'd felt her body first-hand. Though she was beautiful, she was too skinny. Wanting to know about her, he asked, "How did he die? In battle? Is that why you are bitter against royalty and men?"

"What do you mean I'm bitter?" Mina defended. "I never said I was bitter."

"You said that the lycan king was probably as greedy and deceitful as your king. Also, you said that men were all the same, and you wished to go to a realm of all women. Then, you assumed the lycan king would kill you and Sophia rather than deal with you justly." Larus leaned forward and moved to study her. Firelight caressed their skin, giving their bodies a warm glow. She appeared surprised that he'd listened to what she'd said and actually remembered it. "I wish to know what happened to make you bitter."

"I'm not bitter," she said carefully.

"What would you call it?" Larus continued in the same probing tone.

"Disenchanted."

"You also said that the devil had already taken from you," he continued. "So I ask, what happened? How did your father die?"

Mina sighed. "Two years ago my father was accused of conspiring with the Archbishop of York against King

Henry. The king—in an effort to quell the rebellions against him—executed the archbishop and then came after my father. My father didn't wish to surrender, so the king besieged our castle."

"What then?" Larus asked. Feeling a prickling along his neck, he glanced over his shoulder and listened for sounds beyond their campsite. Seeing nothing, he drew closer to Mina, but she wasn't watching him, she was watching the flames set against the dark forest.

"Many of the knights were killed and the king won. He hung my father the same day he stepped into our keep, citing his resistance as proof of his part of the conspiracy." Mina glanced over at him as if suddenly realizing he sat closer to her. She blinked, swallowing nervously. Heat curled through him at the memory of what they'd done, what he could sense she wanted to do again and again.

"Did he conspire?"

"Yes," she said simply.

"And you were left unharmed?" Larus looked deep into her eyes.

"We weren't discovered. One of the loyal knights escorted us from the castle with the servants. The servants ran away, and we went back a fortnight later. Until we were brought here, we lived in the shell of what was once our home." Mina laughed, but the sound held no pleasure. Glancing up at Larus, she said, "I'm glad you're not a nobleman. I've had my fill of those. I'm tired of being lied to and deceived."

"How do you know I'm not?" he asked.

"You would have said."

Larus glanced at the fire, wondering what she would say if he told her he was king of the lycans, born of a noble and ancient lycan family. "Does it matter to you what I am?"

"So long as you're not a king, I think I shall be fine," Mina teased to lighten the conversation. She naturally leaned into him to nudge his side playfully and it felt right that she should do so. Larus set his arm around her shoulders to keep her from pulling away. She stiffened briefly and then settled into his warmth. "The past is the past and dwelling on it won't change it."

He didn't say a word.

"Is your kind always so warm?"

"Yes," he chuckled at the odd question.

"Are there many of you?" Mina made a small movement, nestling closer.

"Yes, there are."

"And do you all look the same when you...?" Mina gave a light shrug and blushed.

"When we shift?" Larus laughed. "No, our faces are as different from each other as humans'."

"I meant are you all shaped the same?" Mina turned pink.

"Being lycan does keep us from gaining excess weight," Larus said, furrowing his brow. "So, yes, in a sense we are all strong."

"Ah," Mina said, nodding. She glanced away, pinker still.

"Oh," Larus chuckled. His arm drew her tighter against him, urging her to look at him. "You wish to know if my—"

Mina gasped and put her hand over his mouth before he could say the actual words out loud. She'd been asking if his arousal was normal in its great size, but as soon as she got closer to the answer, she'd been too embarrassed to continue. He grinned beneath her hand. His tongue darted out, licking her palm.

Peeling her hand back from his lips, Larus began the slow process of kissing each finger before working down the inside of her wrist. Heat built within her and now that she knew what to expect from his kisses, she trembled with longing. She moaned lightly, leaning into him more.

"Come here," he said, nuzzling her ear. He slid his hand around her waist and hauled her forward to sit astride his lap. He caressed her face. "You're beautiful."

"Even if I am human? Despised by the lycan kind?"

Before he could answer, she hurried, "Now it's your turn. What about your family?"

"The last of an old line," he said. "Long, long ago I had three brothers, two sisters, a pack of cousins. Most were killed in the wars with the humans, about three hundred years past."

"So long," Mina said, touching his cheek. "You don't seem to have forgotten them."

"I haven't. I can still see their faces, though their voices have faded from memory." Larus worked his fingers beneath the cloak to feel her hips.

"So that's why you hate my kind?" Mina asked. She could feel his loneliness as if it was her own. "Because they took your family away from you, your whole life? I know that's how I feel about it. I can't blame you for hating us."

Larus shot her an easy smile which belied the seriousness in his eyes. "I don't hate *all* humans."

"Do the vampires hate humans as lycans do?" Mina's eyes cast down, thinking of Sophia.

"Sophia will be fine. Devlin won't harm her. He thinks she's under my protection."

"But, he's obviously a nobleman, why would he care if she was under your protection?" she asked.

"It's our way," he answered, not sure he wanted to say, *because I am king and to displease me is to bring down the wrath of the entire lycan army upon your head.*

"Oh, then you are different from my kind," Mina mumbled.

"Your skin is so soft. I love touching it," Larus said to draw her back to him. His fingers glided up, parting the cloak so he could look at her breasts outlined by firelight. "Lycan women are so hard and muscled. I like your softness."

Mina's breath became ragged. His hands stroked, doing wickedly delicious things to her body. She sighed, and he was glad that she let him.

Cupid paced the forest. It was later than he liked being out, but he'd been traveling all day, trying to find where Larus had taken the women. With great irritation, he finally found their campsite. Keeping himself cloaked with magic, he crept closer to see what was happening.

Larus sat beside the dark-haired sister. Cupid picked a plug of wax from his ears but couldn't hear what they said. Seeing the blonde one wasn't with them, he frowned. Where was the enchanted sister? Why wasn't she there?

Cupid went to his knees and reached forward.

Seeing the glob of wax on his finger, he looked around for a safe place to stick it for later. Not finding one, he wiped it back into his ear, licked his finger, and continued forward. He crawled on his hands and knees, trying to keep the leaves and twigs from rustling as he inched closer. Suddenly, Larus turned, looking over his shoulder. Cupid bit his long lips together to keep from making a sound. The woman kept talking and soon Larus was again paying mind to her. The lycan leaned closer to the woman. Cupid frowned and again inched forward.

"Does it matter to you what I am?" Larus said when Cupid was close enough to hear.

"So long as you're not king, I think I shall be fine," the woman answered.

Cupid's ears perked up. What was this? She didn't know the lycan was king? Aye. He'd have to remember that little tidbit for later. It might serve him well. The lycan king probably didn't want the Lycaon court knowing two humans pursued him.

Cupid grinned. He'd be only too happy to let all at Lycaon know about it. It would serve Larus right. After all, it was he who told all who'd listen about Cupid's good deed.

Bah. Ach.

A bug crawled across Cupid's hand and he looked down in pleasure. Grabbing the giant black insect, he sat back and studied it before popping it into his mouth. It wiggled its way down his throat as he swallowed. Ignoring the couple, he looked for more bugs.

"Oh," Larus chuckled, once more drawing Cupid's attention. He didn't see any more insects, so turned his attention back to the lycan and human. Flinching, he saw them in each other's arms. He gagged, wincing at their closeness. Hideous, ugly, horrible vision. Larus only drew his arms tighter around her, turning her toward him. "You wish to know if my—"

Cupid shut his eyes, not wanting to watch. He forced his ears to listen. Where was the blonde sister? He had to know. After a long silence, the human woman moaned lightly.

"Come here," Larus said. "You're beautiful."

Cupid backed away, not daring to peek at them. His stomach lurched, and he was hard pressed not to laugh. The ugly human, beautiful? Whoever heard of such a thing? She wasn't even passable. No warts or moles. No corns, or boils, or rashes of any kind. No hook nose. Not even a beard upon her chin.

Beautiful? Bah.

"Do the vampires hate human as lycans do?" Mina asked King Larus.

Cupid's tiny ears perked up. He froze, glancing

around the forest but refusing to look at the hideous couple. Vampires. Why was she talking about vampires?

"Sophia will be fine," Larus answered. "Devlin won't harm her. He thinks she's under my protection."

Devlin. That Master Vampire had his human? Cupid shook with anger. Why did Devlin have the girl? He was going to ruin everything. Well, it was lucky Cupid knew where to find this Devlin. Aye, he'd show that vampire what happened to those who meddled in a troll's revenge.

"Your skin is so soft. I love touching it," Larus said. Cupid flinched, turning on reflex to look at them. Larus pulled the woman's cloak aside, baring her horrendous chest. Cupid gagged.

Ach. Larus was right. The human did look soft. Cupid gagged again, close to losing his stomach. Soft and pink and... and...

He was going to retch.

Joyous toadstools.

Cupid turned, running in horror into the forest, not caring if they heard him as he escaped the horrendous vision. Looking back to make sure they were no longer in view, he ran headfirst into a tree, knocking himself unconscious.

18

"I WANT YOU TO KISS ME AGAIN," LARUS SAID ALONG her throat. "I want to feel your soft, full lips on me."

Mina groaned. She knew she should be embarrassed, but she wanted him too much to care. She leaned forward, kissing his shoulder. Then, pulling back, she worked the knot free to bare his chest. The tunic dropped across his waist. She trailed light kisses on him, excrting pressure with her tongue as he had on her. His breath caught and held as she explored his chest. She flicked her tongue over a nipple, causing him to moan with pleasure.

"Lower," he urged. "I want to feel your lips lower and I know you wish to taste me. I can see that you do."

Mina crawled back. Her hands shook slightly as she lifted the tunic from his lap and pulled it up. His erection stood proudly before her. She brushed her lips over the tip. Larus moved his hands to her back, pushing the cloak off her naked body so she was fully exposed. Mina started to pull up, but his hand on her shoulder stopped her.

"No," Larus breathed. "Just like that. I enjoy looking at you."

Mina felt empowered. Larus's hands were on her body, tangling in her hair. The locks were almost dry as they fell over her hands on his thighs. She kissed the tip of his shaft, only to feel him press her head lightly down. She opened her mouth, moving her tongue to taste him and he pressed again. Finally understanding, she took him into her mouth. It was like nothing she'd ever experienced. Her body shook, becoming aroused beyond measure.

"Ah," Larus said. "Oh, yes."

Mina drew back, kissing her lips off him. He pressed her head again, and she again took him into her mouth. He kept pressing, urging her to take him deeper before letting her back up. He did it several times until she learned what he wanted. Her tongue rolled along his mass and her teeth scraped lightly against the sides.

"More," he urged, his tone rough as if pained. "Harder. Suck me in."

Mina did as he requested and his whole body tensed.

She glanced up to see his head had tilted back. She loved the raw, primal sounds he made, the way he shook and tightened. Pulling her lips harder against him, she sucked, bobbing her head up and down. When he came, it took her by surprise. The salty-sweet taste of him filled her mouth as he became rigid. Mina swallowed, lifting off him to study his face.

"That was pleasing?" she asked.

Larus groaned. "Very pleasing."

"Do you want me to do it again?"

"Yes," he moaned, only to chuckle when she smiled and moved as if to take him back into her mouth. "Ah, but not yet."

"Do you need to recover?"

"No, being lycan, I don't take long to recover." As if to prove his point, his shaft filled with his desire, lifting tall. "I want to be buried inside you."

Mina bit her lips with pleasure and crawled forward into his arms. Larus pulled her hips up and began massaging his tip against her. She was ready for him, so hot and needy. When she gasped weakly for more, he gently drew her body down on him. Her mouth covered his, as his thick mass pried her apart. He moved her slowly, kissing her breathless as he built the tension in their bodies with slow thrusts.

Mina learned his rhythm, willingly lifting herself on

his arousal. He released her hips to explore the rest of her body. He massaged her breasts and pinched her nipples, rolling them into erect points.

Mina gasped, breaking her mouth away. She detected Larus's control starting to slip. He kissed a trail down her throat, licking her heated flesh. A growl sounded in the back of his throat. Amber flecked his eyes as the beast took over.

"Turn around," he ordered, his tone hoarse. "I want to be deeper. I want to ride you."

Mina moaned softly. When she took in his expression, she gasped. For the most part, he looked the same, still handsome, powerful. His eyes flickered dangerously. Firelight glinted off his extended teeth. Not understanding, she didn't move but sat impaled upon his lap.

Larus lifted her off him with eager hands. Within moments he had her on her hands and knees before him. She was still wet with need as he drew himself once more to her opening. He grabbed her hips, thrusting inside. Mina cried out in surprise and approval.

Larus rode her, pumping his hips wildly. He told her of how he liked watching himself enter her, liked seeing her body swallow him up. The words were wicked and sinful and they served to arouse her more.

Reaching around he tweaked the sensitive nub buried in her folds, causing an instant tremor of release to hit her. She shook, crying out softly as her hands clutched the dirt. His release followed hers as he stayed buried to the hilt, every thick inch of him quivering within her.

Larus growled a loud, possessive sound. He wanted her thoroughly marked as his. With this moment, he knew that no one would ever touch this woman again. She belonged to him. There was no escaping it.

19

Sophia sat on the bed, staring at the fireplace. Two trails of blood dried on her neck, running from two very distinct puncture marks where Lord Devlin had bitten her. She didn't notice them, didn't care that they were there.

Devlin was gone. He left her to wait, sitting in the burgundy gown he'd given her to wear. Sophia wondered if Larus would like the gown on her. Now that she was clean, she was sure he'd propose to her. She loved him. He was her very air. She sighed, happy in the fog of her dream world.

"Pitiful, pitiful, such the fool."

Sophia blinked, unafraid of the awful, raspy voice. She looked around the castle bedchamber with a smile on her face.

"Ignorant human woman doesn't understand what's happening. Poor, poor fool."

"What did you say?" Sophia asked, her voice mild. "Who are you?"

"A friend, child, a friend."

"Oh, good evening, my friend," Sophia answered. Her eyes drifted off, but the irritable resonance of the voice continued, nearing a cackle as it spoke.

"Aye and deceived by her own flesh. Sent here to rot so that her sister can steal her true love."

Sophia blinked, tilting her head to the side. An awful smell wafted around her, but she didn't notice it. Larus's scent was in her head. His voice was in her brain. His face clouded her eyes until every breath was meant for him. "You know of my lord, Larus? Please who are you? Show yourself, my friend. I would hear of him."

She blinked in surprise as a little creature appeared before her place on the bed. With great effort, the foul-smelling troll walked over the soft mattress, wobbling on his short legs. His fat, crinkled lips stretched wide, nearly encompassing his whole face. Beady black eyes stared out at her, so small they looked like tiny buttons. An overlarge nose hung down. He hit his neck as a gnat bit him. There were several of the little insects swarming around him. He licked his fingers, saying, "Come with me."

Eyeing his dirty brown tunic and pants, Sophia wrinkled her nose as his smell finally penetrated her senses. The foul odor broke through the spell enough to let her notice it. She pulled back. "You smell, my friend. Would you like for me to draw you a bath?"

Cupid grinned as if she'd complimented him. Picking his overlarge nose, he shivered and looked at her in contemplation. He eyed her rosy cheeks and blonde hair but couldn't seem to think of a way to repay it.

"Please, friend, tell me of Larus," Sophia said, softly. "You sound as if you have news of him."

"Come, I will take you to him," Cupid said.

"You will?" Sophia smiled, moving to stand by the bed, ready to follow him wherever he led her. "My heart misses him so. Thank you, my friend, thank you."

20

Mina lay wrapped in Larus's arms, folded in his green cloak. He was behind her, curled around her body. The fire had burned out sometime in the night, but his heat kept her more than warm as she slept.

She picked absently at the gold embroidery along the edge. It was morning. The sun peeked through the tops of the trees. Her legs were stiff, her insides a little sore from Larus's deep touch, but she didn't feel like moving from their spot. She liked the feel of his arm protectively around her waist.

What has happened? she thought in awe. Larus had made love to her for hours, showing her things she would never have dreamed possible.

Finally, feeling as if she must move, Mina squirmed out of his hold. His grip instantly tightened. His voice was soft, steady, and without the remnants of sleep, as he said, "I like you here."

"You're awake," she gasped in surprise.

"Yes," he said, and she felt him brush his nose along the back of her ear.

"I have a confession to make," Mina said, not turning to face him. She liked the feel of his body curled to her back. "Last night, when I was in the stream."

"Yes?" he asked, kissing her neck lightly.

"I didn't feel anything beneath the water." Mina's voice became so soft with embarrassment, it was barely audible. "I don't know what came over me, but I wanted to... be close to you."

Larus's chest jerked as he laughed. "I already know."

Mina gasped, sitting up. She turned, hitting him in the arm. "You knew?"

"I could sense nothing was in the water." He only laughed harder as she hit him again.

"Why didn't you say something?" Mina demanded.

Larus shrugged, an incorrigible gesture. Giving her a lopsided grin, he stated honestly, "I wanted to see what you would do with me once you had me."

"Ah." Mina began to scold him only to blush. She giggled lightly and tried to hide her face behind the veil of her hair. It was one thing to do what they did, another completely to talk about it the next morning.

Larus sat up. Pulling her hair back, he kissed the curve where her neck met her shoulder. He tried to snake his hand around her side, but she stood, taking the cloak with her.

"We need to get dressed," she said, moving to take her dry clothes down off the limb. She pulled them to her chest. "We should start traveling to get Sophia."

Larus nodded. Mina walked into the forest, away from him to get dressed. Thinking of Sophia, guilt assaulted her. She believed Larus when he said no harm would come to her sister, but Sophia did seem to be very in love with him. Even if her sister was cursed, did it make it right for Mina to take Larus?

Mina quickly rinsed in the stream, hoping to wash his smell from her skin. Then, drying off with the cloak, she quickly dressed. Her gown had seen better days, blue was faded and drab but at least it was cleaner than it had been.

Mina walked back toward the campsite, watching her feet, when she heard Sophia shout, "My love. I knew that it wasn't true. I knew my sister wasn't in your arms. Mina would never betray me. I told him as much."

Relief and regret hit Mina at the same time. She stood, stunned, just out of view of the campsite. Larus cleared his throat, sounding uncomfortable. Before he could say anything about them, Mina ran forward.

"Sophia," she called, rushing to hug her sister. Meeting Larus's eyes over her sister's back, Mina shot him a look of warning. "How did you escape?"

Sophia's light brown eyes looked almost wild when she pulled back to study Mina. "I knew you'd never betray me. I told him that. I told him you were good. He said no. He said that you wanted my Larus, that you were trying to take him for yourself. But I knew you'd never betray me. Because we both know what happens to traitors, don't we?"

Mina gasped. There was an underlying threat to Sophia's words. She pulled away. "Of course nothing happened."

"I told him. I told him," Sophia repeated, nodding emphatically. "He didn't want to listen. He talked all night about it. But I knew my sister would never betray me. She's not a traitor like our father. For I would have to hang you, too, Mina, should you take my Larus."

"Sophia?" Mina asked, frightened by her sister's unnatural expression. Suddenly, she noticed the bite marks on her sister's neck. She wore a new gown. "What did he do to you?" Turning to Larus, she demanded, "What did that vampire do to her?"

"Lord Devlin?" Sophia asked. "He did nothing that would be unseemly. He gave me a gown and fed me. He was very kind."

Mina shivered. Larus's eyes were hot on her, livid. She didn't have time to deal with his anger. Sophia needed her. Whatever was happening to her sister, she couldn't drive her further over the edge. For now, whatever she felt for Larus would have to remain hidden.

"So Lord Devlin let you go?" Mina prompted, when Sophia frowned at Larus's possessive stare directed at Mina.

"No," Sophia answered absently, observing Larus with great suspicion. "That was my friend. He helped me away."

"Your friend?" Larus interrupted. "What friend? Where?"

"He was small," Sophia simpered, smiling prettily now that he looked at her. "And he smelled wretched if I recall—like foul milk and rotted animals."

"Long mouth, big nose, small black eyes?" Larus demanded, his face stiff.

"Yes," Sophia said thoughtfully. Then, holding out her arms, she began swaying back and forth, "Larus, my knight, do you like my new dress?"

"Yes," he said, distracted.

Sophia giggled and clapped her hands. "I knew you would. I told Lord Devlin as much."

"You know this foul creature she speaks of?" Mina asked him.

"Yes. Cupid. If that troll helped to free Sophia from Devlin's keep, then he's behind her spell as well." Larus roared in anger. Mina gasped.

Sophia stopped giggling to watch him with wide eyes. "No, my love, it's your spell I'm under. I don't want the troll."

"Come," Larus grumbled. "We need to get off Devlin's land before nightfall. He wanted her until dusk tonight. He'll be upset that Sophia is gone without his permission but can only travel at night."

Larus stormed angrily away from them. Mina shared a glance with her sister and moved to follow. None of them said a word.

"My lord Devlin was quite sweet," Sophia said, eyeing her sister as they walked behind Larus.

Mina nodded. She couldn't help but notice Sophia's words were tinged with a strange insistence. Her sister had been talking nonstop about Lord Devlin for nearly an hour. At first, Mina thought it another ploy to make Larus jealous. But, as Sophia directed all her comments toward Mina, she realized her sister was trying to get her to like Devlin.

"Sophia, I don't—" Mina tried to interrupt. Sophia turned to her, stopping her comments with a glare.

"He's kind," Sophia insisted through clenched teeth. "He'll make a fine husband for you, Mina. Look at this gown he gave me. You will have many like it, I am sure.

Now ask Larus to take you there and leave you. Trust me. I am your sister."

Mina paled. *Husband?*

Larus stopped at that, stiffening. The sisters were too busy staring at each other to notice and Mina collided with Larus's back. Before she even had time to register she'd hit something, Sophia was screaming at her. Mina stumbled in surprise. Sophia lurched forward, shoving Mina in the shoulder as she found her footing. Mina cried out as she fell to the ground.

Looking up at her sister, Mina stared at Sophia's contorted face. She gasped for breath. Her sister's eyes were glazed and her lips shook violently with outrage. Larus automatically moved to help Mina up, not having seen Sophia's attack. Sophia growled and slapped his hand. He turned to her, stunned.

"He is mine!" Sophia hissed at Mina. "Touch him again and I'll take off your limbs."

Mina couldn't move. She glanced at Larus in confusion. Sophia screamed and jumped in front of him so they couldn't make eye contact.

"Look at him again and I'll burn out your eyes," Sophia warned, her features full of venom. Very clearly, she stated, "He... is... mine."

Mina couldn't move. She didn't dare look at Larus again, not with Sophia acting so irrational.

"This is how it will be, sister. Larus is my husband. I will marry him. You will marry Devlin. We will get together for afternoon walks and twice a week to dine. We will both have children and they will play and *you will never look at my Larus again.*"

"Soph—" Mina began.

"No." Sophia screeched at the top of her lungs. "Say he's mine."

"He's yours, Sophia, he's yours," Mina rushed. The words twisted at her heart. She felt pain seizing her, jealous raw pain. She didn't want Sophia to have Larus, and though she knew Larus didn't want her sister, just saying it hurt terribly. Then there was her sister's sanity. It had truly slipped.

"Besides," Sophia said, spiteful. "Look at yourself. You're dirty and thin and he cannot want you."

Mina's eyes swam with tears.

"Sophia," Larus inserted softly.

Sophia's face brightened and she turned to smile up at him. "Yes, husband?"

Larus flinched at the words. Sophia didn't even notice. Mina slowly stood from the ground, dusting off her skirt in an effort not to look up.

"We should go," Larus said. "We need to find Cupid. He can help us."

"Oh, he's already helped." Sophia giggled as if

nothing had happened. "He brought me back to you, my love."

Larus didn't turn. Sophia grabbed his arm and Mina felt jealousy anew when she looked at them walking together. She balled her hands into fists and she had never wanted to hit her sister so much in her life.

Larus frowned, looking to where Sophia clutched his arm. She held him so tight that the blood had stopped flowing to his hand nearly an hour before. Stretching his tingling fingers, he tried to flex his bicep to get her to loosen her hold. He felt Mina behind them and wanted nothing more than to turn and pull her close. He'd been angry that she refused to tell Sophia about them, but now he had to agree it was the best course of action. If he thought Sophia was close to the edge before, she was definitely falling over it now. Cupid's curse was building at an alarming rate.

Sophia sung softly, almost sounding like a child as they walked. She hugged him tighter, sighing heavily, occasionally whispering how much she loved him and how she'd soon be carrying his child inside her. Larus didn't answer. Mina's anger filtered toward him as a distraction. He wanted to toss the blonde sister aside and pull the dark one to his chest. However, he knew it wasn't Sophia's fault. If Cupid had enchanted her to him, she wouldn't be able to fight the spell. Humans were not equipped to fight such magic.

Accursed troll. Larus swore bitterly.

He should have known Cupid wouldn't let things go. The only thing he knew to do was to bring them to Lycaon. Perhaps Rhiannon, being human, would be able to help the women and then he could take Ilar to help him find Cupid. Larus didn't dare bring them to the elders now. It would take too long for them to decide the sisters' fate, and Sophia didn't seem to have time on her side. Every hour she slipped more and more into her dreamlike world and he was afraid it would be too hard to get her out of it.

Lord Malak's was out of the question. With Sophia so enamored, he was afraid Mina would be drawn to the handsome rogue. Malak attracted women like a troll attracted fleas. Not that he thought Malak would take Mina to his bed, as she was marked, but he jealously didn't wish to see Mina throwing herself at the man to spite him.

It was getting late by the time they stopped to make camp. They were close to Lycaon and would be there the next day. He built a fire for the women and hunted for food. It was hard not to go to Mina. He wanted nothing more than to hold her against him, stroke her soft hair, and tell her that he'd take care of everything.

'*Ilar,*' Larus thought, directing his thoughts toward the man using the mind link his kind shared. It took a few times, but finally the commander answered.

'*My king?*' Ilar's words came back at him, connecting their thoughts.

Larus sighed and quickly told his friend what had happened, leaving out the part about his and Mina's joining. Ilar would detect the mark on her easily enough when he met her. He finished his story with, '*Perchance, Rhiannon can help them adjust until I know what to do with them. Lady Sophia is getting worse with each passing hour. I am afraid she will do her sister harm, and herself. I found them, so I am responsible for them.*'

'*I will come for you myself on the morrow,*' Ilar answered. '*We will find Cupid and make him pay.*'

'*Very wel—*' Larus began.

"My love?" Sophia said behind him, interrupting the thought.

'*My king?*' Ilar insisted. '*Larus?*'

'*Until tomorrow,*' Larus directed before turning around. He cut off the mind link as he looked at Sophia.

"What are you doing?" Sophia asked, suspicion in her voice. "Were you thinking of Mina?"

"No," Larus answered. "I was merely listening to the forest to make sure it was safe."

"Oh," Sophia mumbled, though she kept a wary eye on him. Suddenly, her face cleared and she said, "Larus, I..."

Larus studied her, seeing her expression waver into one of confusion. She looked as if she cleared from the fog, only to be slowly sucked back in. "Yes, my lady?"

"I... *help me*," she pleaded. Sophia paused and the cloud came back completely. Her tone became hard once more, as she stated, "I think we should tie Mina up, lest she be tempted to go to you. It's not her fault she can't resist your pull."

Sophia turned to go. Larus took a deep breath. When he found Cupid, he just might kill him.

Mina lay very still for a long time. Sophia slept close to her, gripping tight to her arm. But as her sister's hold finally loosened, Mina inched away from her and sat up. Swallowing, she looked across the campsite. Larus's back was turned, but the second she looked at him, he rolled. His dark green eyes met hers, staring intensely until she almost felt as if he was inside her head, trying to talk to her. She couldn't make out the words.

Mina glanced at her sister. She still slept. Looking at Larus, she tilted her head toward the forest. He nodded in understanding. Mina stood and walked away from the campsite, stopping as she reached just beyond sight of it. It didn't take long for Larus to come up behind her.

Larus hesitated before touching her arm. She shivered, instantly turning into his chest. He gasped softly in surprise but folded his arms around her in comfort.

"What's wrong with her?" she asked, near tears. "Why would a troll do this to her? We have done nothing to deserve it."

"She's enchanted," Larus answered, stroking her hair over her back. "And Cupid does it for revenge."

"Revenge?" Mina repeated, confused. His heart beat steady and strong against her cheek, and he was so warm she shivered to feel his heat. "What did we do to deserve his revenge?"

"You did nothing," Larus answered, pulling her tighter to his body when she would push away. "His revenge is against me."

"You? What did you do?" Mina pushed again and he let her up to look at him.

Larus hesitated and he looked like he wanted to tell her something but was holding back. "I was charged with the task of helping to report him to our council of elders. Cupid enchanted a mortal woman, Lady Rhiannon, from your world and brought her here to the king's castle. It disrupted the guards and put several lives at risk."

"Why would he do that?" she asked, puzzled.

"Because the lycan commander, Lord Ilar, insulted him. Now, he has somehow enchanted your sister to me as revenge against my telling the council of his deed."

Larus's hands stroked absently over her back, drawing around in small circles as he instinctively pulled her body closer. She melted into him. "I'm sorry that you were hauled into this madness."

"I'm not," Mina said, looking shyly up at him. She liked being held by him, had thought of nothing else all day as he walked with her sister. "Not completely."

"Mina—?"

"Will Sophia be all right? Can you help her?" Mina didn't want to delve too deeply into her feelings. She was too scared of what he'd say. He had never confessed more than an attraction for her and somehow she knew he would never lie to her. If he didn't care for her, as she cared for him, then she wasn't ready to hear it.

"Once we find Cupid, we'll be able to discover how to end the spell. I will take you both to Lycaon tomorrow. Lady Rhiannon is there. Hopefully, you will be more at ease being around one of your own."

"Then you will bring us before your king?" Mina asked, growing sick thinking about it. Out of everything, that prospect scared her the most. She trusted Larus would help her sister. But she didn't trust royalty. They only did things to serve their purpose.

"I think you will find he is not so bad," Larus said. He reached up to touch her cheek.

"You can't know what he'll do." Mina thought back

to the night the king's army finally broke through her home. The knights had snuck them from the castle with the servants, but not before Sophia heard them say the king would take the noblewomen as his mistresses, should they be found alive. It was why Sophia was convinced any nobleman who came to Aucester would make them his whore. Mina was inclined to agree. Would this king try to do the same?

"You shouldn't judge every ruler by the one who hurt your family," Larus said. "We aren't like that. We elect our ruler."

"Elect?" Mina questioned, shaking her head. "Every king is elected, most by the sword. Whoever has the most powerful army wins."

"Mina—"

"Please, I don't wish to discuss it further. I fear we will never agree on this point." Mina turned her face into his hand and closed her eyes. "I'll deal with one thing at a time. First, we must help Sophia."

"No," he said, his lids falling over his eyes. "First you must kiss me."

Sophia opened her eyes, staring blankly up at the sky. She could see the silver moon shining its strange light through the treetops. Sitting up, still dazed, she turned to see Devlin sitting next to her.

"Where is Mina?" she asked, her tone even.

"With Larus," Devlin answered.

Sophia's face contorted and her breathing deepened.

"You don't love him," the vampire said. "You know that, don't you?"

"He is my soul," she growled, ready to fight.

"No, he is your obsession." Devlin lifted his hand to caress her cheek. She didn't even feel him, so he pulled back. "I was angry you left me until I smelled the troll's presence. So that's who enchanted you, is it?"

"You must take Mina," Sophia said, hard. "Take her and get rid of her. Or keep her. I don't care."

"You don't mean that," Devlin answered softly. He lifted his hand to touch her lips, running his thumb over them gently. She didn't feel him. His eyes filled with regret and sadness. She didn't see it. "I tasted your love for her when I drank from you. I know you don't mean what you say. You're lost, child, trapped in the spell."

"I do mean it. If she touches him, I'll kill her."

"I feel the remnants of your spirit in you. How I wish I could have met you before this curse," Devlin said. "Before my curse."

"No, I'm fine," Sophia stood, looking wildly about.

"Tell me, where are they? Where's that traitor, my sister?"

Devlin sighed, standing. Slowly, he pointed toward the forest, not saying another word. She wasn't hearing him anyway.

"Kiss you?" Mina smiled and felt a giddy pleasure rise in her chest. Right now, with Larus holding her close, she felt safe. Her arms wound forward, drawing around his neck. She lifted up on her toes and pressed her mouth to his, moaning softly as he parted his lips to her. She was surprised when he didn't automatically take charge and pulled back to see what was wrong. He squeezed her tighter and kept her where she was.

Hesitant, she reached her tongue to taste him. His breath caught and she grew bolder, slipping it into his mouth. Moving her lips, she deepened the kiss, taking control of it as he followed her lead. She slid her hand to cup his face, pulling him closer. She forgot everything, but the feel of his mouth, his body.

"Larus," she said into their kiss. He groaned, setting her back against a tree. He moved against her body, lifting her skirt. She tried to help by pulling the knot at his shoulder. She'd felt the pleasure his body could give her and she wanted to feel it again and again.

She fumbled and gave up, moving her touch lower to lift his tunic. She caressed his heavy length, letting her hand slide over him. Larus pulled his mouth from hers and trembled, biting his lips together to keep quiet. He pressed his forehead to hers and looked deep into her eyes.

Mina pushed on his shoulders, lifting her leg to the side to get closer to him. He growled in the back of his throat. Taking her hips, he pulled her up to rub against his shaft. She was wet, hot, needy, and so very ready for him. Silently, she begged him with her body, trying to keep from crying out, desperate not to wake Sophia.

Larus thrust within her and she gasped, tightly clutching his shoulders. He kept his eyes steady on hers, connecting to her, watching her, letting her watch him. Mina's lids dropped as he began rocking into her in long, eager strokes. The fire inside her built, lighting her blood with a passion only for him. Before long, she started to shake, her sex trembling and clamping down on him hard. Larus didn't hold back, letting his seed fill her as he captured her lips.

"You."

Mina froze, pulling back, as Sophia's voice broke into their private world. She looked frantically around and finally found Sophia standing hands on hips, watching them. Her face was stiff with anger and she was shaking.

"Sophia," Mina began, pushing at Larus. He let her go. Their clothing fell down around them once more. She was weak from Larus's touch and swayed slightly as he moved away. "Listen, I can explain."

"I hate you," Sophia ground out. Mina tried to speak, but Sophia screamed and swung a branch she'd hidden behind her skirt. Larus, surprised by the attack, moved to grab it, but not before it hit him in the stomach, knocking the wind from him. She swung again and hit Mina on the shoulder, knocking her down. Larus growled and jerked the branch away. Sophia didn't care. She let it go and jumped on Mina, wrapping her hands around her sister's throat, trying to strangle her. "You just wanted what was mine."

Mina pulled at her sister's hands, trying to breathe, trying to explain. Larus moved to grab Sophia off, but Devlin appeared by his side and gripped his arm. The vampire shook his head, saying, "She won't kill her."

"She is killing her," Larus swore.

"I've tasted her, read her," Devlin said, his words very calm. "She'll be forced to choose. She'll break the spell. Trust me. Real love will win over enchanted love."

Mina could barely hear them. Her grip weakened on Sophia, but she didn't let go.

Sophia leaned down, crying now. Softly, she said, "He is mine. I love him."

"No," Mina said and she felt Sophia's hands lighten. She gasped for breath, urged Sophia's ear down to her mouth.

Larus lurched forward, breaking free of Devlin. Before Sophia came and interrupted them, it had been wonderful. He couldn't wait to take Mina to his home. He wanted her to meet Rhiannon so that she could see that a human could be happy living in his world, mated to a lycan. Mina had said nothing of feelings, so neither did he.

Now, watching Sophia's glazed eyes, he knew she was deep within the enchantment's thrall. Larus tried to pull away from Devlin, but the old vampire held strong. He couldn't hear what Mina said, but suddenly Sophia fell to the side, sitting in the dirt with a stunned look on her face. Shivering, she looked first at Mina, then Larus, and then the pale vampire. Her eyes were entirely clear for the first time since he'd met her.

Larus didn't move. Mina pulled up on her arms. "Sophia?"

"I... Mina?" Sophia asked, shaking harder. "I... no."

Sophia's mouth worked. Mina reached out and grabbed her. "It's fine. Everything is fine."

Larus made a move forward and Sophia screamed,

clutching Mina behind her back. "Stay away from her, devil."

"Sophia," Devlin stated.

"Who are you?" Sophia demanded. She shook her head frantically when Larus made a move forward. "Where have you taken us? What do you want with us?"

Devlin motioned his hand, stating quietly, "Sleep."

Sophia instantly weakened, falling over. Mina caught her sister in her arms. She started crying. "Is she...?"

"Let her rest," Devlin said.

Mina began to nod, but the vampire disappeared into mist and floated away. Her eyes turned to Larus. She opened her mouth to speak, but a shout sounded, interrupting them.

"My king."

Larus flinched at the sound of his native speech.

"King Larus."

At the same time, Mina and Larus whipped their heads around to look at the guard who came through the trees. The man, dressed much like Larus but in a simpler tunic of light brown, knelt down.

"It is fine," Larus answered in kind.

"What's going on, Larus?" Mina demanded. "Why is he bowing to you?"

The guard looked at her in surprise and sniffed at the air.

"Humans?" the man gasped, looking back to Larus for confirmation.

"They are under my protection," Larus stated.

The guard nodded. His words stunned, he said so the women could understand, "My king, we sensed a vampire."

Larus flinched.

"King?" Mina asked weakly, clutching Sophia closer. Her eyes filled with tears. Larus looked at her, his expression begging her to understand, but knew she couldn't see it in her confusion.

"What are you doing in the forest?" Larus asked. He'd planned on telling Ilar not to reveal his station earlier with the mind link, but Sophia had interrupted the conversation and he forgot to pass the order along. How could he have told her he was king of the lycans? She didn't trust royalty and would think he purposefully deceived her. It didn't matter now. Now it was too late. She knew and by her look she wasn't happy.

"Lord Ilar sent us to attend you," the man answered. "The others are at your campsite. We've brought provisions."

Larus nodded. He looked over at Mina and

commanded the man, "Lift the blonde lady and take her back to camp. Make sure no harm befalls her."

The man nodded and made a move for the unconscious woman. Mina gripped her sister closer. The man sniffed, his eyes shifting to a light gold.

"Do as I say," Larus ordered.

"Yes, my king," the man said. Mina protested, but he pulled Sophia up into his arms, ignoring the feeble punches she dealt him. He walked through the forest to the campsite. Mina moved to follow him. Larus's hand shot out to grab her.

Mina froze, jerking to be free. He didn't let her go. Larus waited until the man was gone, before saying, "Mina, we need to talk."

"Is that a royal decree, your majesty?" she demanded. She jerked harder and he let her go. "I've heard enough of your lies. I've nothing to say to you."

With that, she walked away, following her sister. Larus stared after her, his heart feeling as if it were ripped out. He'd tried to sense what she was feeling, but she cut him off, blocked her emotions from him. It was as if a slab of ice was placed inside him, chilling him to the bone.

"Mina," he said. It was too quiet for her to hear. Falling to his knees, he repeated softly, "Mina."

MINA HUGGED SOPHIA CLOSE, KEEPING A SHARP EYE on all the men sitting across from them at the campsite. They all watched her curiously, seeming to sniff in her direction when they thought she wouldn't notice. They exchanged strange looks, speaking in a language she couldn't understand. They were dressed as Larus. Arms and a shoulder were left bare, making no mistake that these men could part from their clothing at a moment's notice. Calves were naked, some cross-strapped with leather bands coming from short boots.

Inside, she trembled. King Larus. It couldn't be real. But, as he came walking into the campsite several minutes after she did, Mina knew it was true. The men instantly stood and bowed to him. He waved them down, his eyes moving to meet hers. She purposefully hardened her heart, glancing away into the flames.

"If we shift, we can carry them back to Lycaon tonight," one guard suggested. "We detect a vampire is near."

"Lord Devlin," Larus stated. Mina again glanced at him, but he wasn't looking at her, he was focused on his men. At the name, the lycans seemed to relax their guard a little. They began talking once more in their native language and Mina could but watch, trying to decipher what it was they said.

After a moment, the men stood. Mina blinked, hugging Sophia closer. Larus came over to her, his face impassive. "We shift to take you to my castle. There you will have a warm bed, food and a bath."

Mina looked up at him. She couldn't speak. The feel of him was still too fresh on her body.

Larus knelt. "Do you understand that we will shift to carry you?"

Mina nodded, not afraid of that. Behind the king, the men pulled out of their tunics, unashamed as they brandished their nakedness about. Mina turned a bright shade of red and quickly looked away from the naked men. Larus glanced over his shoulder and chuckled. Some of the guards noticed her reaction as well. They, too, laughed, murmuring amongst themselves at her strange human modesty.

Mina didn't move until she felt another presence close to them. Larus reached for Sophia, saying, "Fallon will take good care of her."

Mina didn't have much choice as Larus lifted Sophia from her and placed her carefully onto a black wolf's back. Sophia sighed and automatically cuddled into him. Mina stood, dusting off her hands. She looked at the men turned lycan. They were picking up their clothes with their mouths.

"Ah, here," she said, moving hesitantly forward to gather the clothing from them. Their wolf eyes blinked at her, but they set the clothing down. Several nodded at her, grateful. Mina gathered the tunics and boots up into her arms. Behind her Larus growled. The men looked at him. Those that could took their clothes back up before she could reach them. Others looked at her expectantly until she dropped them back onto the ground.

As the wolves ran off into the forest, she moved to follow them, trying to keep an eye on the one who carried her sister. Feeling a nudge at her leg, she glanced down. She'd know the tan wolf anywhere. She stared down into Larus's green eyes and shivered. He nudged her leg, motioning his head for her to climb onto his back.

"I can walk," Mina protested weakly. Larus growled,

low in his throat, and again motioned for her to climb on. "What would your men think, majesty, if you were carrying a *human* on your back? I'll walk."

Mina tried to take a step. Larus jumped in front of her, bracing himself on all four paws. His fur lifted on his back and his head lowered in warning. She was a little scared of him at that moment.

"Fine," she grumbled, relieved when he relaxed. He turned. She glanced around, picked up his clothes for him and moved awkwardly to sit astride his back like she would a horse. When her feet dragged along the dirt, she shifted her weight and lay down as Sophia had been placed. It felt strange being close to him when he was like this, surrounded by soft, warm fur. She tried not to think about it, tried not to admit that she didn't care about his shifted form, that it didn't bother her.

She held on as he moved, feeling the strong flex of his muscles beneath her. Soon he was sprinting, racing through the forest. Mina watched trees blur past. Her heart pounded with excitement. It felt as if she flew. Without realizing it was there, a smile curled her lips. She held on tight, never wanting to let go.

24

THE SILVER MOONLIGHT COMBINED WITH THE LIT torches along the battlements. The lights made it easy to see Lycaon as they approached from the forest. The battlements circled around the bailey, disappearing in the distance. Square turrets were built in intervals along the outer face, standing tall as lookout towers. A stone house encased the gated entrance. Lycaon Castle was grand, like no other Mina had ever seen. Only a few guards stood within the outer bailey, between the inner and outer gates.

Larus took her through the front gate into a bailey before a tall castle. Stopping in the yard, he waited while Mina dismounted. She was too busy looking around to notice Larus had shifted and stood before her naked. He cleared his throat and she jolted in surprise at the sound.

Blushing, she handed him his clothing. He artfully swung the tunic around his body and knotted it.

"Where is my sister?" Mina asked. Larus moved as if he would take her arm. She pulled back.

Frowning, he didn't try to touch her again, as he walked through the inner gate. "She has been taken abovestairs to my personal wing."

"You put her with you?" Mina questioned, suspicious.

Larus's frown deepened and he turned his hard eyes to her. Through tight lips, he stated in a low voice as not to be overheard, "I put her in a guest chamber in my personal area, not in my personal chamber."

"Oh," Mina said, almost feeling bad that she had jumped to such a conclusion. Then again, he had lied to her about being royalty. The knowledge of what he was stiffened her resolve against him.

"You will be staying in my personal chambers," Larus stated, once more walking ahead of her.

Mina shivered at the possession in his voice. She glanced over the empty bailey yard on her way to the castle entrance and debated whether or not to follow him inside. It was eerie in its nighttime quiet, as if abandoned. The gate behind her was wide open. She could at least try to make a run for it. She saw a subtle shift in the shadows and made out the faint outline of a soldier standing at attention as the king passed. Perhaps that wasn't the best course of action. He'd only catch her before she made it beyond the outer gate.

So the king expected her to stay with him as his mistress? Even as the thought of being in a soft bed next to Larus brought her untold pleasure, she cursed him for the very idea. What had happened to her pride that she would even consider being compliant in this?

"I will stay with my sister," Mina said quietly, as they came into a long hall. A raised platform for the nobles was on one side and lower tables lined a good part of the stone floor. The hall was empty, dark but for a gentle orange firelight.

Larus sighed, looking annoyed. "Mina, the men smell my mark on you. They know you are my..."

"Mistress," Mina filled in, tight lipped.

"Lover," Larus said, his voice dipping softly at the word.

"It's the same thing," Mina answered.

"One night." Larus nodded to her and motioned to the stairs.

"What do you mean, one night?" Mina asked. She hesitated, but in the end moved to follow his gesture.

"You may stay with your sister this one night," Larus answered. "I'll tell everyone you take care of her. They'll understand."

Mina walked up the stairwell, very aware of how close behind he followed her. She frowned. "I don't care what they think, majesty. Their thoughts are no concern to me."

"Mina," he warned. They reached the top of the stairwell and he pulled her arm to stop her from walking down the wrong hallway. Mina stiffened, but he merely redirected her and let go. "I didn't tell you who I was because I knew it would harden you to me."

"Well, your highness, you were right. I am hardened to you." Mina was tired. She knew she was spoiling for a fight. Exhaustion, the fatigue of walking, the worry for Sophia—it all finally got to her.

Larus stopped. He looked over her features and lifted his hand, gently moving as if to cup her cheek. She stiffened. Instead of touching her, he moved his hand beside her arm and pushed open a door. Then, merely nodding, he turned and walked back down the hall. She watched him disappear down the hall that she'd first tried to go.

Sighing, she stepped inside the room. Sophia slept on the bed. Her sister looked peaceful in her dreams and Mina realized it was the first time since coming to the magic realm that Sophia looked like her old self. The large fireplace burned brightly, casting the gray walls in a golden light. Her stomach growled, but she ignored it.

The room was spacious, doubling as a sort of bower. Beautifully carved high-backed chairs with plush cushioned seats were near a long, slotted window. Next to the chairs was a carved table of dark wood. Strange rugs were lined beneath the window, made from what she assumed was wool.

Too tired to think of anything, she walked over to the bed and collapsed atop the soft mattress next to her sister. If she never got up again, it would be too soon. Within seconds, she let the darkness consume her, falling into a deep and much needed sleep.

25

To Mina's surprise, Larus didn't come for her after that first night. She spent the day in the chamber with Sophia. They bathed, slept, ate, slept some more. Lady Rhiannon, a very beautiful human who Mina remembered as being mated to a lycan commander and the victim of Cupid's mischief as well, brought them a change of clothing. The long sleeved undertunics were much like the ones they wore back home, but the long rectangle of soft material that served as a dress looked more like Larus's tunic, as they wound it around their bodies and pinned them at the shoulders. Mina was surprised to find how comfortable the outfit really was.

Lady Rhiannon, or Rhian as she asked them to call her, didn't stay long that first day, understanding their need for rest. After a second night of sleep, she came back, offering to escort them around the castle grounds. It was a lovely place, richer than any castle they'd ever been to, and impressively big. King Henry's palace was nothing compared to King Larus's.

Mina couldn't help but notice Sophia's pale face as they walked. There were many fine-looking men at Lycaon, many who showed an interest in Lady Sophia. Rhiannon admitted that the guards referred to Sophia as the unclaimed mortal and had sought an introduction. Rhiannon had told them no.

Sophia didn't seem to notice the hot eyes and curious stares that were directed at her. If she'd been so inclined, she could have had her pick from any of the unmarried lycans in the Lycaon court. Mina would have been jealous except for the fact that the only hot stare she wanted to see belonged to the lycan king.

Rhiannon said the men wouldn't dare to think of Mina now that she bore King Larus's mark. They all knew her to be the king's woman. Mina balked that her deeds were so widely known, but it seemed of little importance to anyone else.

Sleep had done much to clear her head in that regard. She might have been too unfair in judging Larus. In hindsight, she saw how her words would have kept him from telling the truth. She did harp on about royalty and he had tried to broach the subject, suggesting perhaps that lycan royalty wasn't so bad. Top that with the fact that humans had killed his entire family, and it was unlikely he'd seduced her merely for a bed partner. The fact he wanted her, a human woman, had to be torture enough for his pride. She wanted to apologize to him, but Lady Rhiannon told her he left the palace with Lord Ilar to find Cupid.

They went to the hall to dine with Lady Rhiannon. There, a horde of little winged fairies took notice of the new women and buzzed around their heads, checking them out. They all wore beautiful gowns that glistened like stars. The pretty creatures furrowed their brows and wrinkled their naturally upturned noses in distaste. Mina frowned, not understanding their buzzing chatter, but could well make out the impertinence in their giggles.

Sophia was still dazed from her enchantment and wasn't so immune to seeing the magical creatures about her head. She paled all the more, appearing extremely uncomfortable as she hunched down in her chair.

The swarm of pesky fairies began singing a childish tune the women couldn't understand, as they moved to encircle Mina's head like a floating crown. Some of the lycan men laughed. Mina was no longer able to ignore them either.

"Ah, off with you," Rhiannon scolded in annoyance,

swatting lightly through the air with her hand to scatter them. "Don't mind them. I'm convinced they're related to fleas, only prettier."

"Oh," came a high-pitched huff as one of the pretty fleas overheard the comment. She stuck out her tongue and flew off to report Lady Rhiannon's words to the others. Rhiannon didn't appear too concerned.

"They only tease you because you're... you know, with the king." Rhiannon smiled, tactfully.

Sophia made a weak sound of annoyance and pain. Mina had her sister's assurances that she wasn't jealous of what had happened in the forest and in fact didn't want Larus for herself. Sophia was having a hard time coming to terms with her embarrassment over the enchantment. She was a proud woman, who clung even more desperately to her freedom now that she had it back.

Mina hated to see the hardening in her sister's eyes, but it couldn't be helped. She only hoped that, in time, Sophia's heart would soften.

"They look at me as if I'm naked." Sophia frowned, her eyes turning over the hall with contempt. Many lycan men stared back at her, waiting for her eyes to stop favorably on them. They didn't.

"I saw some of them naked," Mina admitted in a low voice, hoping to cheer her sister up. Sophia couldn't sulk about the enchantment forever—at least Mina hoped not. Her sister was never one to be told what to do and having her will take away had to be a traumatic blow to her ego.

Rhiannon laughed.

Sophia's eyes got wide. "Mina!"

"They part from their clothes to shift. I nearly died when they all undressed as if it were nothing," Mina said to the two human women. Sophia's lip twitched at little, though she quickly controlled the look with one of even temper.

"I did the same first time I saw it. Can you imagine? There I was, standing in the yard, waiting for my husband to give some order to the men, and with a sudden swing of the arm, they all drop their clothes and before me stood an army of naked, handsome warriors. Thankfully my husband is understanding, because my jaw dropped and I stared overlong." Rhiannon laughed louder. She was a pretty woman with her long curly blonde hair and stormy blue eyes. But it was more than the physical that made her attractive. It was the love in her gaze when she spoke of her husband and her life at Lycaon. She was truly happy.

Mina chuckled, understanding her shock. She'd only seen a small group of soldiers and couldn't imagine a whole army. She wondered if the men were all shaped differently. If she knew Rhiannon better, she would have asked.

"The women strip like that as well. It makes me glad to be human. I don't think I could stand bare in front of all these eyes," Rhiannon continued. Her face fell a little, as she admitted, "not that they would notice."

"What?" Mina questioned, diplomatically. "You're beautiful, of course they would notice. How could they not?"

Rhiannon chuckled. "They are lycans, not humans. Once Ilar claimed me as his, they look at me with no more interest than they would show another man. Really, after the stunning blow to the ego goes away, it will be a relief. When I first came here under Cupid's spell, they all wanted me—every single last one of the unmarried ones. I'll take one man's attention to a whole army's, to be sure."

Sophia made a derisive sound at the mention of Cupid's name. "I can't wait until we are back amongst our own."

Mina's eyes fell. She didn't want to think about going back, but Larus had never mentioned anything about wanting her to stay with him. He might not even wish for her to. To be fair, she never gave him an opening to talk about what he wanted, how he felt. All she knew was that, without him, she felt cold and alone.

"At least our men use proper deceit to woo a woman to their bed, not magic," Sophia continued. "Honestly, Rhian, I don't see how you bear it."

"It's not so bad here," Rhiannon defended, looking a little hurt by Sophia's words. She picked up her goblet and sipped.

Sophia, even though bitter, had the good sense to draw back her tone. "I meant such things are not to my nature. Your life is one to be envied, but it's not for me. This realm or my own, the truth is, I've never been suited to being a wife."

"You mean, you," Rhiannon paused, looking strangely at Sophia, "you fancy women?"

Sophia and Mina, both in the process of drinking, chocked and coughed. Rhiannon laughed at their looks.

"No." Sophia denied when she could again breathe. "Truthfully, I may someday take a lover, but I've no wish for a husband."

"Sophia," Mina gasped at the bold claim.

"I say nothing that you yourself have not done, dear sister," Sophia quipped. "I, however, will be more practical in my choosing. I'll decide on a lover like I would a good stallion. Find a man with good teeth, decent bloodline, a fine gait and superior form. Someone wild and strong, but also someone I can break to my will with the right training. Then, when broken, like a good horse trainer, I'll sell him for a profit and get me a new one."

Mina paled. Her sister couldn't be serious. A few men at the tables below must have heard her, for their eyes lit with desire and their stares became overbold. Some even reached to feel their teeth, baring them. Sophia ignored them all.

Rhiannon only laughed harder. "Mayhap you should stay in this world Sophia. From what Ilar has told me, women are scarce and many men would be willing to fight for the honor you spoke of. If you like, we can have a tournament."

"And risk being mesmerized to a vampire or doused with magic so I lose my will?" Sophia shook her head in firm denial. "No, I'll take the human realm. At least there the odds will be fair. No enchantments, no mysteriously swirling eyes. I've been forced into love twice and I swear I will never try it a third time."

26

THE THICK FOREST OF RED TREES BEYOND LYCAON Castle broke open to a long field of rolling grasses. The sun shone brightly in the soft purple sky, as the shifted Larus, Ilar, and Fallon sprinted toward Fenris. Cupid's cave was on the way to Malak's home. Ilar and Larus would be stopping to pay the little troll a visit. Ilar had been to the troll's house once before when his wife was enchanted. Fallon would go on to Fenris to request Malak's presence at Lycaon.

Malak guarded the portal and would know when, and how, to send the humans back through—or how to find someone who could. Larus trusted Malak with his life and would trust him to see Mina and Sophia safely back. The very idea of sending Mina home tore at him, but Larus had seen well the look of mistrust and hate in her eyes the last time they spoke. She'd actually flinched when he'd tried to touch her cheek—as if he could hurt her. He would lay his life down if she so demanded it. After her rejection, he knew the only hope he had of breaking free of her spell over him was to send her as far away as possible, back to her world where she belonged.

A few hours passed as they ran and the field gradually thinned. They neared a rocky path wide enough for all three lycans to run side by side. A green dragon flew overhead. They ignored the fierce creature and the fire it spouted out across the sky. The rolling field turned into small hills. The small hills grew into larger foothills. And, as the morning turned into afternoon, the foothills finally rose in the distance to show a range of glorious mountains.

It was evening by the time they reached Cupid's cave. The lycans saw easily through the darkness as if it were daylight. Their eyes flashed with golden slivers. The moon was half full, shining the most exquisite silver over the land.

Fallon nodded as Larus sent him orders with the mind link and continued on to Fenris. Larus and Ilar stayed shifted, leaping up the rocks toward Cupid's cave. The flowers along the pathway flattened and torn if they'd been shredded underfoot. Bundles of dried bouquets and baskets full of discarded darts were strewn down the mountain.

Larus stopped as they reached Cupid's cave, glancing at Ilar. There was no door, no welcoming indication that anything lived in the dark hole. Due to the unbearable smell wafting from within, it became necessary to shift back to human form so that it didn't permeate so strongly into their sensitive noses.

Standing naked, the two men looked at each other and then to the hole. Ilar frowned, saying through the mind link, '*I have no wish to go in.*'

'*It smells as if something has died,*' Larus returned, wrinkling his nose in disgust. '*Too bad we don't have water. We could flood the varmint out.*'

'*Yes, or at least bathe him before you went in after him,*' Ilar smirked.

'*Why me?*' Larus frowned.

'*Because, you do this for your heart,*' Ilar smiled, knowingly. '*You do this so Mina will have comfort and peace, and she won't be frightened. You do it to protect her. You do it because you must.*'

'*It is so very obvious?*' Larus let loose a heavy sigh.

'*Only to one who knows you,*' Ilar smiled. '*You do love her, don't you?*'

'*Yes.*' Larus nodded, the word an echoed whispered

in his head, sad, drawn, and heartbroken. '*Since the first moment I laid eyes on her.*'

'*You would face hell for her?*'

'*Yes, I would,*' Larus answered, without stopping to think.

Ilar grinned and motioned toward the cave hole. '*There's as close to hell as we'll likely ever be, my king.*'

Larus shot his old friend a bemused glance, fearing that he may be right. He stepped forward toward the opening, displeased with this grim task as he tried not to breathe in the foul stench. A stern look upon his face, he called down, "Cupid, show yourself."

Silence radiated from within.

"Cupid," Larus barked. "Come out."

Again silence.

"I don't think he's here," Larus said, standing and moving away from the cave. "But it's too hard to be sure. The whole place reeks of him."

"Should we wait?" Ilar asked. "He'll be back. He won't be able to resist staying away from his home. Trolls are known to always return to the same spot."

"Yes," Larus said, upset that he'd have to wait to confront Cupid. "You wish to hunt our supper or guard this hole?"

Ilar automatically shifted back into wolf form. His gaze filled with a liquid gold, slivering until the color overtook his eyes. His face elongated slightly, growing with fine dark brown fur, as his mouth parted to show dangerously long, sharp teeth. He growled rhythmically in the back of his throat, a sound that sounded oddly like laughter. *'You stay. I'll hunt.'*

Cupid hid high on the mountain, watching the two lycans camping before his home in wait for him. They were in wolf form, making them all the more dangerous. He frowned, pacing back and forth behind a boulder, scratching thoughtfully inside his ear for wax. He was nearly out of cloaking magic and needed to get inside his cave.

Unfortunately, the lycans would hear him coming and he had no desire to be caught by them. If not for his need to meet with the other trolls at the campfire to brag about what he'd done and hopefully redeem some of his reputation, he'd have been inside the cave and already within their grasps.

What was Larus doing outside his home? Without the human women in tow? It made no sense. He shouldn't have been able to lose the women, not unless...

Cupid grinned. The only way Larus could be free of the blonde human was if he'd tied her up, or even better if he killed her. He bit his long lips to squash his laughter. The dark one would be angry for sure at that. She might even try to kill Larus for killing her sister.

Oh, aye. This was a grand turn.

If Ilar was here with Larus, it only meant the dark sister was at Lycaon Castle. Cupid's squat legs moved, climbing the hard way over the mountain so he could use his magic to slip undetected over to Lycaon to see for himself what was happening there. With Larus here at his cave waiting, the troll should be perfectly safe going to the lycan's keep.

27

"Lady Rhian," a guard said, bowing down before her as the three women sat outside on a bench talking. He had a dark complexion with matching dark hair and eyes and was smaller of build than some of his brethren. His gaze turned to Mina, "My que... ah, Lady Mina."

Mina looked at him, choosing not to understand what he'd been about to say. For all she knew, she had it wrong anyway. But, how did he know her name? Well, it would seem in the field of gossiping tongues, their races were the same.

The man turned his handsome dark eyes toward Sophia, his voice becoming a low growl, as he said, "Lady Sophia."

Sophia flinched and said nothing. She turned her eyes away toward the wall. The man didn't look disheartened by her slight. In fact, he looked even more enamored by her.

"Tal," Rhiannon acknowledged, not bothering to hide her humor at his stare toward Sophia.

"We would like to tournament to be Lady Sophia's lover," Tal stated.

Sophia gagged. Mina instantly put a protective hand on her sister's shoulder. Rhiannon's smile faded.

"No," Sophia croaked, instantly standing.

"But...?" Tal looked confused. "She said she wished to judge for the position. It has been decided. Only those with good teeth will compete."

"Come Sophia, let's go," Mina said.

"Did she not say she wished to pick one out?" Tal asked, staying with Rhiannon. Mina didn't hear what Rhiannon answered, as she pulled her sister away.

Weakly, Mina said, "It is, ah, flattering they wish to tournament for you."

"To be their whore," Sophia said, her voice hoarse. She walked toward the stairs leading toward their shared room. Mina moved to follow her. Sophia stopped, holding up her hand. "No, Mina, let me be alone for a moment."

What had happened?

Cupid seethed, frustrated, as he stormed along the battlements of Lycaon Castle. Damn Devlin for his interference. Things had been going fine until that vampire kidnapped the blonde mortal away.

Cupid had been so sure the women would have done something—anything—to King Larus. But, no. They sat in his home, not fighting, not screaming, not dead, not anything. They didn't even go after the lycan king as they should. And what had happened to his enchantment? How did the disgusting blonde mortal break his magic? Larus wasn't mated. The blonde human wasn't dead. He saw no other way for the enchantment to end.

But, aye, it was gone.

This he wouldn't stand for. Cupid's foul body shook with outrage. No one broke a troll's enchantment before it was to end. No one.

"Mina, you must choose your path," Lady Rhiannon said. Sadness touched her eyes and Mina understood that the woman had formed a friendship with them and liked the bit of the human world of which they reminded her. Rhiannon didn't want to lose that. "And Sophia must choose hers. Just because she wishes to leave, doesn't mean you have to. I have a sister left behind, who knows nothing of this world. I miss her, but admittedly, we weren't as close as you two are."

Mina sighed. She did like Rhiannon. In a few short days, she was more friend than any other woman, aside from her sister. "Sophia is my only family. She's my responsibility. We're all we have."

"Lady Rhian." A passing guard nodded in greeting as he walked by. Then, turning to Mina, he said, "My queen."

"All right." Mina frowned when he left, uncomfortable with the title. "Why do they keep calling me that?"

"It happens sometimes. They don't use our language and, occasionally, they mess up some of the words so try not to take offense," Rhiannon said. "I nearly brained a man who insisted on calling me Ilar's possession, until I realized the sod meant the word mate. Believe me, if they're angry or trying to mock you, you'll see it well enough in their faces. They don't hide such things well when you learn to read them."

"I'm not offended, just curious as to why they keep referring to me as royalty," Mina said quietly. "I'm not... married."

"Perhaps they mistook the word to be a title of respect for your position as Larus's woman." Rhiannon smiled as more guards walked past. They bowed their head in acknowledgment of the women but, beyond politeness, didn't spare another look.

"I wish they wouldn't," Mina admitted, her heart squeezing in her chest with uncertainty. Would Larus think kindly of a human being called such? "It's embarrassing enough to have them know I sinned without having them speak a reminder of it."

"But I had the impression you liked Larus," Rhiannon inserted, keeping her voice low. "These people are kind and honest."

"I'm not questioning their kindness," Mina said. "Or their honesty."

Well, she had questioned Larus's honesty, but she understood why he didn't tell her who he was. It was only a title after all and men should be judged on merit, not title. Mina had spent so long hating royalty, blaming them, venting her frustrations out at them that she hadn't stopped to think about it.

Rhiannon frowned. "Is it because they're different that you don't wish to stay? Is it because Larus is a lycan? I know it can be strange, especially for us being raised as we were in the mortal world, but I swear they have more honor than that of our bravest knights. They live by a chivalrous code we could never hope to find elsewhere. The shifting, it's strange to be sure, but can you not see past it? There are advantages to a man who can protect you as they can."

"That's the thing. To survive in this world, we must be under a man's protection." Mina thought of Sophia. Her sister wanted less to do with men than she did before they came. Sophia would never take a man for protection and Mina couldn't blame her.

"Is that so bad, to be protected by a man?" Rhiannon asked. "If we were to marry back home, we'd be more like property. Here we are equals. We can't do some of the things that they do such as fighting, but we have our minds. They respect their women, listen to what they have to say, even go so far as to follow a woman's advice if it's sound. If a lycan pledges himself to you, he'll never stray, never cheat or lie. If you bind yourself to one, he'll lay down his very life for your happiness. His life becomes your own—his thoughts, feelings, everything given to you freely. And, in return, he'll know how you feel, accept everything about you—each quirk, each flaw, each doubt. Don't let prejudice stand in the way of what you feel inside."

"I think them an impressive people," Mina said softly. "And Larus's shifting has never bothered me."

Rhiannon arched a brow in question at that statement.

"Oh, all right," Mina said, making a guilty face. "I did

think him the devil—for a short time, mind you. How could I not? The priests speak of such creatures as being instruments of hell. But, if what Larus has told me is true, then perhaps that belief comes from the old wars. Larus never acted the devil—well, not in a way I minded."

"Larus won't let anything happen to you," Rhiannon affirmed. "He'll protect you both until you find mates. He has claimed you as his wards. You've seen how the men look at Sophia. She'll have her pick of any of them— each of them fine, brave men."

"And if she doesn't find one she likes?" Mina asked. "What then?"

"There are other races." Rhiannon smiled, hopeful. "Elves are said to be very compatible to humankind. I haven't met any, but surely someone will strike her. The vampires are compatible in the physical sense, but they are a little daunting in my opinion. I mean, I know the lycans have a strange taste for blood, but at least the lycans eat food and can go about in sunlight."

Mina hummed softly, thinking about it. The idea did have merit.

Larus's head perked up from his paws. They still waited outside Cupid's home. Turning to Ilar, he asked, '*Did you hear that?*'

'*Lycaon,*' Ilar answered. They both stopped to listen to the faint call.

'*Cupid's been detected there.*' Larus motioned his head that they should go. Both lycans jumped up. Taking off at a sprint, they hurried their way home.

"I want to stay," Mina said to her sister, coming into their shared room. She'd given her time alone, affording herself the same leisure to think about her future. Rhiannon was proof that a human could be truly happy in this world and, if he would have her, Mina wanted to be happy with Larus. It was a gamble, he might not even want her in such a permanent way, but she had to try. For her heart, she had to try. "I've thought about it and I think we should stay here."

"Mina," Sophia said, keeping her mouth open as if she would say more. Slowly, she shook her head.

"There's nothing left for us in our world," Mina insisted. "Larus has put us under his protection. It's more than we could hope for—"

"You don't mean that," Sophia said. "How could we possibly stay here? Why?"

"Adventure," Mina said weakly. She knew her sister still raged about what had been done to her. She couldn't help that. But, here, even if Larus didn't keep her, they would be treated better. They wouldn't starve, wouldn't freeze. They wouldn't be alone. "You wanted to see the world, well here we are. This is more world than you'll ever find back home. Let's stay. We have nothing to go back to, no one. We can adjust to the magic, the creatures. They said that humans tried to harness magic in the past which means we can use magic to get us by. We can learn."

Sophia trembled slightly before stiffening her back and her resolve. "I have no wish to stay in this place, Mina."

"You won't even consider it?" Mina asked, going to her. She rested a hand on her sister's shoulder. Sophia shrugged it off. "For a short time at least? See if it agrees with us once we know more?"

"You can't know what it's like to be violated as I have been," Sophia said, her eyes sad. "You haven't been through what I've been through. You've found something, someone. I've got nothing here, but you. That vampire drank from my neck, Mina. He drank my blood and I let him, was *happy* to let him. He looked into my eyes and I would have let him do anything he wanted to me. He could have said to hold still while he cut off my limbs one by one and I would have let him."

"Did Lord Devlin hurt you?" Mina asked when her sister paused. "Did he...?"

"No, my maidenhead is intact," Sophia's eyes were filled with tears and she swiped at them almost angrily. "But he could have is my point. I don't want to be here. I don't want there to be a next time. I had no will, no fight in me. And I loved Devlin. When he looked at me, I loved him more than myself. And when I saw Larus, every breath I took was for him. I felt love Mina, as true as I'm ever likely to find it, truer than I ever want to feel it again. But it wasn't real. I don't love Larus or Devlin, but the feelings I had for them were so real. It's like my heart has been ripped out, only there was no one to rip it, no one to mourn. I don't have a name or a face. I don't have someone to fight for. All I have is the emptiness left behind now that the love is gone. I never want my happiness, my very sanity, to be dependent on another's feelings for me. I don't wish to be that helpless."

Sophia shook. Mina hugged her tightly to her chest, saying, "I won't let anything happen to you. I promise."

Sophia's voice dropped into a whisper, "I would rather they'd raped my body instead of my mind. I had no control over myself and I almost killed you because of it. I never want to feel out of control again. I have to leave this world. Don't you understand, Mina? I can't stay."

Mina nodded slowly. She did understand, and it was her duty to protect Sophia. She was the eldest daughter and, beyond that, she loved her sister very much. She couldn't let her go back alone to face the evils their world had in store for them. If Sophia was to starve, then Mina would starve by her side. "You're right, Sophia. You can't. I won't either. I'm sorry I asked it of you. I can't let you go back alone. I won't abandon you. You are my blood."

29

LARUS STOPPED RUNNING AND LIFTED HIS HEAD INTO the air. He shot a meaningful look at Ilar who slowly nodded in agreement. Turning, they headed for the trees at a slower pace. Cupid was near. They smelled his foul stench. Creeping low to the ground, they edged forward into the forest.

"Ach." Cupid grumbled to himself, pacing near a sand pit. Larus and Ilar both knew the pit to be a sinkhole. There weren't many in the forest, and usually they weren't deep enough to pull a grown man under. "Damn Devlin. Damn Larus. Damn the mortals."

Larus and Ilar shared a look of concentration, staying hidden.

"End my enchantment, will they? Bah." Cupid said, pulling hard at his ear. He kicked a twig into the sinkhole and watched it float on top. "Damn Ilar and his human. Damn them all. I hate them, hate them. They should be suffering, not I. Ach. Bah. They sit in his home, not fighting, not dead."

Larus urged his body to shift, letting the tingling sensations come over him slowly so he wouldn't make a sound. Ilar did the same.

"Toadstools," Cupid cursed. His foul body shook with rage. Suddenly, the smelly troll stopped his tirade. A strange light entered his beady eyes as a smile stretched his wide mouth. "No one breaks a troll's enchantment before it's to end. No one. They must pay, must suffer. I will take the sisters. Aye, I will take them away from Lycaon. There will be no love for the ugly mortals. I will curse the castle with death to all that find love within its walls. Aye, death."

"Cupid," Larus stated, hard. He stood to tower over the troll, arms crossed over his chest. His eyes glittered with anger that the troll dared to threaten his home, his people, *his Mina.*

Cupid squeaked in horror and tried to run. Ilar jumped high into the air, landing on his feet. Hands on naked hips, he looked down at the troll. "Going somewhere?"

"Out of my way," Cupid sputtered. "You have no reason to detain me. I've come to gather sand."

"We know what you did, Cupid, and I intend to tell the council you broke their orders," Larus said. "You will be severely punished."

"I broke nothing, lycan." The dirty troll picked at his nose in agitation. The two lycans grimaced as he sucked a snot covered finger into his mouth. "The council ordered me not to bring over any enchanted mortals and I haven't done so."

"What about Lady Willamina and her sister, Lady Sophia?" Larus charged. His chest rose and fell and he wanted nothing more than to strangle the creature and be done with him. His duty as king kept him from acting so rashly. An aggressive act might send the trolls and other creatures of the underground into a desperate frenzy. It was the cause they needed to start another war of the races. "I heard just now from your own lips that you brought them here."

Cupid looked confused and pondered what he'd been saying when the lycans came forward. His sickly green skin flushed and his nose quivered as it lifted and fell. Reluctant, he admitted, "Aye, I brought them. But I didn't bring them enchanted. I followed the council's decree. The mortals were not enchanted. You were, King Larus. It was you I struck with my dart. The enchantment was on your head, so begone from me, lycan. I've broken no order."

Cupid made a move to walk around Ilar. The commander stepped in his way. The troll kicked him in the shin. Ilar winced but didn't fall over. With lightning reflexes, Larus darted forward and lifted the troll off the ground by the back of his dirty pants. He held him up and away from him, not wanting to get much closer than that. He was too angry at the moment to mind the horrible stench the troll emitted.

"We should slaughter you for the threats against my kingdom, Cupid," Larus growled, letting his gaze shift in warning.

"But you won't kill me, will you, lycan king?" Cupid snorted, laughing. His little legs kicked furiously through the air as he tried to get free. "Your beloved council would have your head for taking justice into your own hands."

"It's time to end this nonsense." Larus frowned. He looked at Ilar. Ilar nodded his head. "State your terms. What do you want?"

"Let me go, lycan," Cupid said, obviously aware that he'd been caught at his game. His feet kicked and under the stench of his body, Larus could detect the troll's fear. "Let me go and I'll give my word that my revenge against you in this matter is over."

"I still must tell the council of your actions," Larus stated.

"Do and I'll make it right by the humans," Cupid said. "I'll take them all back and hide them where you'll never find them."

Larus and Ilar exchanged looks.

Cupid turned his attention to Ilar. "*All* the humans."

Ilar stiffened. Larus closed his eyes.

"Do you agree?" Cupid asked. "Or should I tell them to get ready for a journey? How will you lycans feel, seeing your hearts taken from you?"

"Agreed," Larus said. "End your revenge and leave us. I won't tell the council and I'll leave you here alive."

"Agreed," Cupid chuckled, his voice dripping with disrespect and loathing. "And remember never to cross a troll, lycan. Now let me down."

Larus looked at the sink pit. Odds were it wasn't deep enough to drown him, but it would detain him long enough for them to get back to Lycaon before Cupid could get out.

"You need a bath, troll," Larus stated. Ilar grinned. The king swung Cupid around to the pit. The troll squirmed with renewed force, cursing violently.

"You swore to leave me alive," Cupid said.

"Oh, yes, I did," Larus agreed. "And I'm a man of my word. When I leave you, you will be very much alive."

"Larus," Cupid yelled. The king dropped him, watching him plop into the sinkhole. Instantly, the troll's body sank until it reached to his chin. The tips of his fingers stuck out the top.

"Smells better already." Ilar grinned at Cupid. Then, in warning, he said, "Stay away from my mate, troll."

"Toadstools," Cupid said. "Bah. You deserve your ugly mortals. Curse you all."

Larus and Ilar shifted, making a run for home. Cupid had given his word and wouldn't break it. This matter of revenge was over—until the next time the lycans crossed the miserable little man.

30

"My queen," a guard said, bowing down to Mina in the courtyard. She'd been looking for Rhiannon, to tell her that she had changed her mind, that she and her sister would be leaving the magic realm for home. She also wanted to ask the woman where the portals were. At the man's words, she forgot her mission and stiffened.

Mina took a deep breath, eyeing the man. "I'm not your queen."

The man blinked at her words, his mouth opened but no sound came out. He looked over her shoulder and then back to her. Slowly, he nodded and walked away.

Mina sighed heavily, watching him.

"You must forgive them. They do not know your abhorrence for royalty."

Mina spun around to see Larus. Her eyes widened as

she looked him over. He wore a simple blue tunic, blending in with the guards. Her eyes roamed over his bare chest, his strong arms. She wanted to touch him, to have him touch her. Nervously, she glanced around the courtyard, noticing several of his men watching them. "Larus."

"We found Cupid. It's over," Larus stated. He searched her, probing her.

Mina shivered and glanced at the ground. "He's dead?"

"No," Larus answered. "We called a truce. I gave him a deal he couldn't refuse."

Mina took Larus at his word, trusting when he said it was over that it truly was over. "And what of us? What will happen to us? To Sophia and myself, I mean."

"What do you want to happen to you?" Larus studied the woman before him. She held his heart within her grasp and didn't seem to realize it or care. He had dared to hope, dream even, that she would come to love him, want him, need him. Hearing her denial about being the queen, it was all too clear that she would never accept him. His heart squeezed in his chest, dying a little.

"Sophia would like to go back," Mina said.

Larus looked at the ground. After the spell she'd been under, Larus couldn't blame Lady Sophia. "And you, Mina?"

"I," she hesitated, searching his expression. Larus waited for her words, desperate to hear them. Quietly, she finished, "I must go back as well."

Larus was sure the rest of his heart died at that moment and he would never feel it beat again. "Very well, if that is your decision. Lord Malak arrives from Fenris shortly. I'll make arrangements for him to take you back with him. There is a portal near Fenris and he'll make sure you get safely across it."

"I'm sorry," Mina said. "I know how you feel and I'm sorry to have caused you embarrassment in front of your people."

Larus had been wrong. He felt pain—raw, aching pain where his heart was. Without saying a word, for nothing would come past his tight throat, he nodded and turned, needing to be alone in his bedchamber.

Mina watched him walk away from her. He didn't say anything, not really. He was going to let her go without a fight. She wanted to strike him. But, how could she? He had promised her nothing.

31

A ʀᴏɢᴜɪsʜ sᴍɪʟᴇ ʟɪᴛ ᴏɴ Lᴏʀᴅ Mᴀʟᴀᴋ's ᴅᴀʀᴋ features, as he walked into Lycaon's main hall to greet his old friends. His long hair spilled over his shoulders in raven black waves, nearly touching his waist. The unmated women cast their eyes to him in instant invitation, knowing he would likely take several to his bed as he did on each visit. His gray-green eyes lit with mischief as he winked at them. Malak hardly took anything seriously, except his duty.

His chest was bare as he never fastened his tunic over his shoulder, preferring to let it lay about his trim waist. Larus and Ilar were sure he did it to attract the women. It worked, for he had an overabundance of females vying for his companionship.

"Malak," Larus said, unable to force pleasure to his face. "Thank you for coming."

"I hear there are more mortal women running about your keep," Malak said, striding forward to grab Ilar's drink from in front of him. He tipped the goblet up to a maid, grinning as she giggled. He drank his friend's wine and set the goblet down empty. "Ah, how could I stay away from such news? Tell me, Larus, how is it Lycaon gets all the new females and Fenris is overrun with the same ones? I have half a mind to find Cupid and insult him myself if it will bring pretty women to my door."

Larus merely grunted, saying nothing. Malak glanced at Ilar in question. Ilar shook his head slightly, refusing to answer the concern with the king present.

"Your man was very vague in the details, my king," Malak said, leaning against the table. He drew his finger lazily over the top. The maid he had tipped the goblet to came forward with a drink for him and he took it, smiling handsomely for her. When she left, he continued, "All he would tell me is that there were two mortal women, and you wished me to take them to Fenris with me."

"To the portals," Larus said. "It's my wish that you see them safely back to their home."

"Ah," Malak frowned. "I had hoped that you wished me to mate with them. From your man's descriptions, I've had fantasies aplenty of two beautiful sisters."

"You are a pig."

All the men turned around, just then realizing they spoke in the human tongue. It seemed they'd been slipping into it more and more lately as if mutually agreeing to practice it. The whole of Lycaon had been using it, out of respect of Lady Rhiannon and now the two new ladies.

Larus eyed Sophia. She was much changed from the pliant, lovesick woman she'd been. No longer were her eyes soft. The few times he had gone near her, she had cringed before stopping to glare—as if such a look could scare him away.

"My lady," Malak drawled, pushing up to bow before her. "I can assure you. I am quite the wolf."

"And I am quite the hunter," Sophia answered, her voice lowering. "I do enjoy skinning wolves. Speak of my sister or me in such a way again, and I'll be more than happy to turn your ugly hide into a rug."

Larus and Ilar exchanged amused looks. Sophia stormed off. Malak glanced back at them in horror.

"By all the lycan *that* wench is the shrew you wish for me to escort to a portal?" Malak grimaced. "I can see why you do not wish to go yourself. Pray, let me kick her through it with the bottom of my boot."

"That is Lady Sophia," Ilar said.

"She is under my protection, Malak," Larus added,

his tone stern. "I'd have your pledge to guard her and her sister with your life. I'll entrust them into your care from the moment you leave until they are safely through the portal."

"If you ask it, it is done," Malak said instantly, very serious. He placed a fist over his heart. "I give you my word of honor."

Mina couldn't leave her room. Her swollen red eyes were embarrassing, but it was her heart that refused to let her see Larus. If she did, she would humiliate herself. Burying her face in the mattress, she couldn't find the will to move.

"Lord Malak has arrived," Sophia said, coming into the chamber. She frowned, making a horrible face as she said his name. "He is the most insufferable toad. The nerve of him."

"I'm sure he is fine," Mina managed to get out, dashing her tears on her sleeve.

"Mina?" Sophia asked, going to her side. Mina bounced a little as Sophia's lightweight pressed down on the mattress. "What is it?"

"Nothing," Mina said, hiding her features.

"You love him, don't you? It's not lovesickness. You

really do love him," Sophia said. Mina began crying harder, nodding her head frantically. "Have you told him?"

"I... I can't," Mina said. "There's no point. We're leaving forever."

"You wear your heart in your eyes, Mina," Sophia said. "I was a fool not to have seen it before now. I've felt the love you have. Only it's no spell that put yours there, is it?"

Mina sniffed. "Don't. I... I don't want to talk about it."

"My heart was broken by a troll's magic. Nothing can be done for that. But you, Mina, your heart will be broken by your own actions." Sophia stood. She turned and moved to the little slit of a window to look out over the distance. "I can't live knowing my selfishness took you from your happiness. You deserve happiness."

"I must take care of you," Mina said. "It is my duty as the eldest."

"No, Mina, no," Sophia said, so softly Mina had to strain to hear it. "I'm too old for a caretaker. You've done your duty by me, but it is time you looked to yourself. Go to him. Tell him how you feel. If he'll have you, stay. If he won't have you, then he is a fool. Larus may seem many things to me, but a fool is not one of them."

"Sophia...?" Mina said, wanting to say so much. Her

heart was full, yet torn. She wanted to stay, wanted Larus. "Won't you reconsider? Stay with me. Stay here. You don't have to marry. You're the king's ward. You'll have food and shelter and we'll be together. You won't starve or freeze. Please, consider it."

"You know my reasons," Sophia said. "I can't stay, and you can't go."

"Soph—"

"No," Sophia interrupted. "I said go to him. Now."

Mina heard the wavering of her sister's voice and surged off the bed to hug her. "I love you."

"I know," Sophia said. "Go tell it to the man who doesn't."

Mina sniffed, nodding. She stood, helpless and confused, as thoughts raced in her head. Sophia patted her cheek before urging her gently toward the door. "It's all right. I promise. Go, Mina."

Mina searched for Larus, unable to find him. By the time she gave up and climbed up the stairs to go back to her chamber, she was shaking. Watching her feet as she stepped up, she almost ran into Larus's chest as he was coming down.

Gasping in surprise, she pushed back, startled. Larus grabbed her before she fell down the stairs. He curled his strong hands around her arms, not letting go even as she was steadied.

"Ah," she said, her heart hammering in her chest. Her eyes darted up to meet his. He looked tired but was so handsome. His dark blond hair was pulled back from his face. The green of his tunic brought out the green of his eyes. She shivered, trying not to look at his mouth, trying not to think about his kisses when she needed to concentrate. "Larus... I mean, my lord."

At her words, he tensed. Without answering, he took her arm and helped her up the stairs. Her legs shook badly.

"I was looking for you," Mina said weakly. His look wasn't conducive to confessing how she felt.

"I was in my chambers trying to sleep," Larus answered.

"Trying?" Mina asked, concerned about him.

At that, Larus turned to study her, his eyes softening by a small degree. The corner of his mouth twitched, though sadness ruled his expression. "I was unsuccessful."

"Oh."

"You wished to speak with me?"

"I—" She couldn't meet his eyes. Wringing her hands, she asked, "Can we go somewhere private?"

Larus looked around the empty hallway in question. They were some place private.

"Sophia," Mina explained weakly, motioning toward their shared chamber.

Larus nodded. He guided her arm toward his bedchamber. Mina followed him in, waiting as he shut the door. The room was simple, not what she'd have expected from a king. There was a large soft rug—not of fur, but wool. The bed was huge with a simple green coverlet over the top. It had dark wood furniture, a trunk, a large fireplace with chairs. A game board stood in the corner, ready for use. She wandered over to it, fingering one of the delicate game pieces.

"Sophia tells me Lord Malak has come to take us to the portal," Mina began softly, hoping to discover something about what he thought.

"Yes," Larus answered. He crossed over to the fire. "You're trembling. Are you cold? I sometimes forget how fragile humans are. Would you like me to light the fire?"

Mina was touched by his concern but shook her head. She couldn't take her eyes off him. She thought wistfully, *'What I want is for you to hold me.'*

Larus's eyes whipped to her, a strange expression on his face. "What did you say?"

"I-I didn't speak," Mina said, confused. *'I said I want you to hold me, kiss me. I want you to make love to me, Larus, please. I need you to.'*

"You want me to hold you?" he questioned, unsure. He took a step forward. Mina's mouth fell open. There was no way he could have known she thought that. "You said you wished for me to hold you, kiss you, and… make love to you."

"I didn't say that," Mina thought in horror. Her heart stopped beating. Her mind raced. *'How did you know that? Oh, blessed saints. He knows. He knows. He knows. He knows. Oh, God, please let him say something. Please. Let the floor open up and swallow me whole. If he doesn't want me, let me die right here. I don't want to live. Why doesn't he say something?'*

"I'd like to know something," Larus said, his eyes carefully shaded. "It's been bothering me. Cupid's spell. He said that it shouldn't have been broken. How was it broken? What did you whisper to your sister to make her stop her attack?"

'I couldn't speak, but if I could have I would have told her I love you with all my heart,' she thought. *'That you were what made me whole.'*

Larus rushed forward, pulling her into his arms. He searched her face. "Do you mean it?"

"Mean what?" Mina squeaked, near tears. It felt good to be held by him, but she didn't understand what was happening. "I didn't speak."

"Do you love me?" Larus asked, softly. He pulled her length to his.

"I..." Mina hesitated. She thought about lying, about saving a shred of her dignity. But he touched her and she couldn't think. The truth came tumbling out. "I love you, Larus. I want to stay with you for as long as you'll have me. I'm sorry, so sorry. I didn't mean to judge you because of your station. I know I'm human and an embarrassment to you in front of your men and I can't hope that you could feel the same way, but—"

Larus's mouth crushed down on hers, silencing her. His lips parted, eagerly claiming hers. When she was panting and breathless, he pulled back, his eyes shining with love for her. "I'll never let you go. I love you, Mina. You are mine. Only mine. I choose here and now that you are forever my lifemate. Never shall it be undone."

She saw the golden light in his gaze purpling and cementing, knowing he'd done something to bind him to her. She smiled, pleasure flooding her heart as she accepted him completely. "Larus, did...? Did you just ask me to marry you?"

"No," he said, coming down to claim her mouth. Mina gasped and pulled back, her gaze unsure. *'I didn't ask. I just did it. I'm never going to let you get away. You are mine, Mina—my queen, my wife, my mate. You are my heart.'*

"Larus," Mina sniffed, beginning to cry anew. "But what about your people? I'm human. Won't they... I can hear you in my head."

'Yes, and I you. We are bound.'

"That is going to take some getting used to." She lifted up, kissing him deeply. There was no more need for words. Larus pulled her onto the bed next to him. The only blight in her happiness was that Sophia would be leaving her. But, who knew? Perhaps Sophia would find what she had. It wasn't over until it was over.

Mina felt Larus's spirit inside her, heard his thoughts, felt what he felt. His love only reflected the depth of her own, making it all the sweeter. He'd heard her words in his head and they'd warmed his blood, brought his heart back to full life. Pleasure and happiness, sweet and pure, burst from him, spreading over her. This was what Rhiannon was talking about. Only with his true mate would he be able to read her thoughts as if she were a lycan. They were connected.

"Forever," he said, echoing her thoughts back to her. "We are forever."

The End

New York Times & *USA TODAY*
Bestselling Author

Michelle loves to travel and try new things, whether it's a paranormal investigation of an old Vaudeville Theatre or climbing Mayan temples in Belize. She believes life is an adventure fueled by copious amounts of coffee.

Newly relocated to the American South, Michelle is involved in various film and documentary projects with her talented director husband. She is mom to a fantastic artist. And she's managed by a dog and cat who make sure she's meeting her deadlines.

For the most part she can be found wearing pajama pants and working in her office. There may or may not be dancing. It's all part of the creative process.

Come say hello! Michelle loves talking with readers on social media!

www.MichellePillow.com

facebook.com/AuthorMichellePillow

twitter.com/michellepillow

instagram.com/michellempillow

bookbub.com/authors/michelle-m-pillow

goodreads.com/Michelle_Pillow

amazon.com/author/michellepillow

youtube.com/michellepillow

pinterest.com/michellepillow

JOIN THE EXCLUSIVE CLUB!

Join the Pillow Fighters' Reader Club to stay informed about new books, sales, contests, giveaways, exclusive content, preorders and more!

michellepillow.com/author-updates

THE SERIES CONTINUES...

CUPID'S FAVOR

Cupid's Favor
Paranormal Fantasy Romance
Naughty Cupid Book Three

Beware of trolls bearing favors.

When Lord Malak saves Cupid from a sandpit, the troll is honor bound to settle the life debt or risk being called upon later—even if the lycan noble insists he doesn't want any reward for the deed. Simply breeding the man's goats isn't enough to repay such a price. No, for this he needs something more. Knowing the perfect gift to be revenge, Cupid delivers the one thing that seems to aggravate Lord Malak the most—Lady Sophia.

After being kidnapped and drugged by the horrible Cupid, Lady Sophia wants to go home—to a place where magic doesn't exist and there's no chance of being eaten by a dragon. But most of all, she wants to be rid of her escort, Lord Malak. The charming lycan swore to protect her and see her safely home, but it seems fate and a little troll have other plans.

Excerpt

Bah. Accursed luck.

Cupid brushed sand off his arms, mumbling to himself. He frowned, not liking what he had to do, but a debt was a debt. His beady, black eyes flashed with an inner fire. He might be many things, but a troll who reneged on a life debt was not one of them.

Lord Malak had pulled him from the quicksand and saved his life. Now Cupid owed him a great favor in return, even if the lycan noble insisted he didn't want it. If Cupid didn't give it to him now, he knew that someday Malak could come back to call upon him, and that was something he refused to accept. It was bad enough he would be forced to help a lycan, but to be in Malak's debt? No, that would be worse.

So, what to do? No small feat would repay a life debt. He couldn't merely breed Malak's goats for this one. He needed something big. He needed something grand.

Love?

Cupid nearly gagged as the thought popped into his head. He hit himself on the ear to get it out. A gooey clump of sand fell out instead. Love? Why in all the realms would he think of love? He hated love. He hated the way people looked while they were in it. The way they talked, acted, swooned, and kissed.

Bah. Ach.

Cupid hacked, spitting sand on the ground. The grains were everywhere, rubbing into every crease, chaffing his flesh. Worst of all, the sinkhole had cleaned him of his most glorious stench. He hadn't bathed in decades. It would take him forever to get that smell back.

Damn King Larus for throwing him into the sinkhole and Lord Ilar for letting him. So what if the two were bitter about what he'd done to them? The trolls still teased him about helping Lord Ilar and Lady Rhiannon fall in love, and now he'd be ridiculed for King Larus and Lady Mina as well. Could he allow another blemish to surface on his name?

Bah. No.

No, love was no way to repay a debt to the lycan who saved his life. Ah, but hate. Now there was a real idea. Hate was much better than love. Hate made your blood boil and your heart race. It made you feel alive and gave you purpose. Aye, hate. He'd have to watch Lord Malak very closely and figure out whom he hated the most.

Then, Cupid would bring that creature before Lord Malak to destroy.

Hate. Cupid rubbed his gnarled, wrinkled hands together. A smile spread over his flat, wide lips. Now this was a good idea. Besides, what better way to squelch his undeserved reputation as a matchmaker than to help a lycan find his revenge?

To find out more about Michelle's books visit www.MichellePillow.com

PLEASE LEAVE A REVIEW

THANK YOU FOR READING!

Please take a moment to share your thoughts by
reviewing this book.

Be sure to check out Michelle's other titles at
www.MichellePillow.com